EMMA

EMMA

Jeff VanOudenhove

JAVO
PUBLICATION

Westfield, MA

JAVO Publication
Westfield, Massachusetts 01085

This is a work of fiction. The characters, places, and events portrayed in this book are either the product of the author's imagination or are used fictitiously. Any similarity to real persons, living or dead, business establishments, or events is coincidental and not intended by the author.

ISBN: 979-8-9918888-0-6

Library of Congress Control Number: 2024924027

Cover design by Jeff VanOudenhove

For Emma & Patti

Acknowledgments

I would like to thank my editor, Elizabeth Kelly, who is never afraid to run out of ink when marking up my manuscript to turn it into a coherent story.

I want to thank the members of the WhipCity Wordsmiths, whose support and honest feedback are so greatly appreciated during my writing process.

Thank you, Trudy Knowles and Nadija Mujagic, for the invaluable suggestions on the chapters you read and how to better present them.

I would like to extend my sincerest gratitude to the members of the Psychological Thrillers Book Club Facebook group, starting with the administrator, Mark Jenkins, who is incredibly supportive of newer and lesser-known authors, and others who have tirelessly supported and promoted my work, including Jamie Smith, Sorell Locke, Sara Avery, Brittany Hammes, Fabian Harmsen, Katie Moore, Michelle Godard-Richer, Paige Sorensen, and many, many others.

My thanks to Keeley Webb for taking the time to offer a selfless suggestion for a cover blurb.

And finally, to my family and friends who have supported and encouraged me to continue writing, including Kathy, Billy, Carol, Amy, Loni, Warren, and others too numerous to name. Thank you all.

On to the next.

A Fresh Start

Don't judge me by what you hear from the other girls; they don't even know me. But they will. They'll see I'm not that bad. It'll take a lot of work on my part, but I'll get them to like me. People always do. There's just something about me; I'm a very likable girl.

At my last school, I was everybody's friend. I didn't ask for that burdensome privilege. It just sort of happened. I don't know what it was, but they all confided in me. With everything. I knew their fears and their aspirations. I knew their deepest, darkest secrets. Even the staff were always overly friendly to me. Teachers tended to favor the smarter students, and with an IQ upwards of 127, I was their prized possession. Most times, I used it to get my way. Let's face it - why would I have been granted such a gift if I wasn't supposed to exploit those with lesser intelligence? It's not that I looked at them any differently. Not really. It was more of a game to me. Heck, even some of my favorite teachers were as dumb as a box of rocks. That only made it easier to manipulate them. It's how I learned some of *their* secrets, too. Luckily, they knew none of mine.

I transferred to Bellamy High School six months ago after my mom's company relocated to Massachusetts. It was my senior year, I had just turned eighteen, and it was supposed to be a fresh new start for us. The timing couldn't have been better. Things were getting a little crazy back home in Cameron County, Pennsylvania. My mom's deranged ex-boyfriend was getting paroled after spending eighteen months in jail for attempting to murder her. He'd done the same to two other women before he met my mom. It's too bad they neglected to step forward until *after* my mom's case. They could have saved my mom and me from a whole lot of abuse, though mine was only from the outside looking in.

In addition, my history teacher, Mr. Blouth, one of my favorites, I might add, went missing for weeks before authorities later found his half-eaten body in the forest. Apparently, he'd been mauled by a black bear when he went out for a hike one afternoon and became its dinner. His wife, Dr. Meredith Blouth - the principal at our school - was devastated. I'm sure you can imagine. They'd been married thirteen years when authorities notified her that her husband ended up as bear food. And to think, those were the same trails I used to wander around as a kid. It's scary to think what could have happened if I'd ever come across a bear.

Then, there was that other little matter. You see.., I knew a secret of Mr. Blouth's that I had to keep quiet; there was no sense bringing it to light after his death. He'd gotten a student pregnant and planned to leave his wife. That wasn't something you shared with just anyone - especially in our little township of Gibson, where rumors spread faster than wildfires. The whole place probably would have imploded. I'm only telling you now because you seem trustworthy. I *can* trust you, right? Good. Anyway, I guess the whole bear encounter meant he left his wife, after all - only not the way he intended.

Now, I know you're probably wondering what happened to the girl. Well, she dropped out of school after news of Mr. Blouth's death was announced one morning during homeroom. She was only in her first trimester, so nobody knew her secret. Well, nobody but me. But, as I mentioned, I knew *everybody's* secrets. Don't believe me? Let me give you some examples.

My old neighbor from back home, Mr. Nub (yup, that was his name), liked to shoplift. I'd caught him a few times at the grocery store, pocketing candy bars while waiting in the checkout line. I thought he had a bit of a sweet tooth, the way he piled the packages of cookies, the pints of ice cream, and the individual-size fruit pies into his basket on any given shopping trip. I wondered how he stayed so thin until I learned of his wife's condition. She was bedridden, unable to lift her six-hundred-fifty-plus-pound frame. Even if she were to miraculously stand up, she couldn't leave the house. She was too large to fit through the doors. I often wondered if Mr. Nub realized he was helping to contribute to his wife's massive size. Then again, maybe that was the point. Maybe he was trying to get the poor woman to croak from heart disease so he had an excuse to move on with his life. Death is easier than divorce.

Then there was Duda Lawicki. Duda wasn't his real name; it's just what people called him after he became the quarterback of the football team at the start of our senior year. His real name was Dudley. Can you believe that? He told me his parents were high when they decided to name him after some actor who starred as a bumbling alcoholic named Arthur in some movie from the 80s. Anyway, Duda only became quarterback after he'd intentionally ratted out his "best friend" and *previous* starting quarterback, Trent McNamara, for cheating on his finals our junior year. Nobody knew who the rat was. But *I* knew. Duda told me himself when we went out on our first - and only - date. As I said, people confided in me. It's too bad Duda was all hands and a little immature for my tastes. He was really cute. I wasn't really interested in him any-way. I only agreed to go out with him to make someone else jealous. Not that it would have mat-tered, for reasons I don't care to discuss. Anyway, my mom and I moved a month and a half later, so we left it all behind us.

Yeah, for a small town, Gibson had a lot of se-crets. I knew a fair share of them - some I wish I didn't know. But this was a fresh start for me and my mom. I could leave all those secrets behind. Including mine. Things would be different here. A whole new town with all new people. More impor-tantly, all new secrets to learn; secrets I could hopefully use to my advantage.

Chapter 1

Liza's Story

I met Liza Faraday on my first day at Bellamy High. We immediately hit it off. She wasn't like the other stuck-up Swifties who decked themselves out in sequin-splashed, concert tour tee-shirts of their favorite singer. I swear their sole motivation was to enlist all others into their cult. Instead, Liza leaned more toward the darker side, an attitude matching her naturally straight, jet-black hair that fell past her shoulders. She had an eyebrow piercing over her left eye as well as a nose ring through her septum. She wore dark eye shadow and black eye liner which brought out her light-brown eyes, a feature that instantly attracted me to her. Not in a lesbian way, mind you – I'm totally into men - but there was something about those eyes that caught everyone's attention. I wasn't immune to their allure. If I ever decided to swap teams, Liza would be my reason. She'd be tops on the list of mountains I wouldn't mind conquering. Anyway, in my new world, Liza's complicated secret was the first shared with me - and may still be the worst I've heard.

They say monsters aren't born, they're created. In Liza's case, it's her inner demons that are her monsters, and they were most definitely created.

An only child and daughter of a single parent, Liza garnered all the attention her mother could give. From kindergarten through seventh grade, she was home-schooled, where her mother took great pride and care in her daughter's education. Unfortunately, during that time, in her most innocent of years, the education Liza received wasn't limited to only academic studies.

From as far back as Liza could remember, she and her mom were very close. *Very* close. She didn't think much about the always-open bedroom door where her mother would often parade around the room naked. Her mom's random announcements about "snuggle time" never bothered Liza, where her mom would squeeze tightly against her on the couch, smothering her with hugs and soft kisses on the cheek for a lengthy period. Liza thought it was perfectly normal when her mother frequently asked her to sleep with her in the same bed. She didn't find it strange or unusual when her mother insisted on bathing her, though the extra inspections for cleanliness were a bit uncomfortable. For Liza, it was all just routine.

By the time Liza was eleven, the sexual abuse had escalated beyond the tenderness and sweet caresses. She claims she doesn't remember the specific details, only that it got worse. But, like a good little girl, she always did what her mother asked because she loved her mother and wanted to make her happy.

I asked her once how she wasn't weirded out by it all. She told me there were times she felt shame and that a lot of it seemed dirty and gross, but that her mom had a way of making everything seem normal and right.

When Liza was thirteen, her mother enrolled her in the public school system, and having been so abused, Liza found herself sneaking stares at the other girls in the gym locker room, admiring their developing bodies, wanting to caress them as her mother had taught her, and wishing they would return those same gentle caresses. Her interest in boys was non-existent. When the other girls noticed her sexual, undisguised glances, they became uncomfortable with the "new girl." Rumors spread. She became an instant outcast. When the staff heard about Liza's obsessive glares toward the other girls, she was instructed to shower and dress in privacy, only allowed access to the girls' locker room after the last student had vacated it. Because of that, Liza was allowed to arrive fifteen minutes late to her next class, which meant all eyes were upon her as she entered the classroom, her hair still dripping wet from the water that washed away the dirt and sweat but could never wash away her shame.

By the next year, her first in high school, the atmosphere was completely different. And although the staff at Bellamy High School was more progressive and socially understanding of students' sexual orientation, for Liza, the damage had been done. She would forever be that creepy outcast who couldn't stop staring at the other girls in the locker room. So, if being an outcast was Liza's course in life, she decided she would begin to dress and act the part - a part scripted for her by her intolerant classmates. But it wasn't Liza's fault; the blame rested on her filthy mother's shoulders. Only, nobody knew that. That was Liza's secret - one I would hold onto as tightly as I held onto our friendship.

Chapter 2

The Games People Play

I stood beside Liza's locker, waiting for her to gather her books from the mess she maintained within. While she rummaged through the shambles of her own creation, I couldn't help but stare across the hall at the perfectly sculpted cheerleader dolls shaking their pom-poms at every popular boy that walked by - and they weren't holding their pom-poms if you know what I mean.

"I don't get it," I said, while Liza fought with freeing her Economics notebook from beneath her World History text. "Why all the fuss over those four? They can barely form complete sentences."

"It's their blonde hair," she replied without breaking her focus, "and their over-eager willingness to put out."

It was unfortunate, but she wasn't wrong. The adage *"Blondes have more fun"* was never more true than at Bellamy High, where all the boys perved over the fairer-haired females while spurning those of us cursed to live our days being scrutinized because of the cruel misfortune of the dark hair we lived with since birth. High schools were all the same; this one just seemed worse.

"I get that," I responded, pulling a lollipop from my mouth and squinting over the top of it as if it somehow made me invisible from the Barbie quartet's line of sight. "It's just that, you'd think the guys could control their raging hormones for the brief three minutes between periods."

"Well, when three minutes is all you get," Liza replied, "and in their case, the longest any of them could last, you have to make the most of it."

"Good point," I said, recommitting the lollipop to the inside of my cheek while checking to see Liza's progress with her seemingly eternal struggle.

"You know, you should probably think about organizing your locker a little better," I added. "It might eliminate all these problems you seem to constantly have."

"Hey, some people pay good money to go to the gym to workout," she replied. "Don't be so critical about how *I* choose to exercise; this is free."

I rolled my eyes. "You could always join the cheerleading squad."

"Oh please."

Liza gave one final tug, freeing her book from the clutches of her cluttered locker that doubled as a trash compactor. If only she could have managed that feat twenty seconds earlier.

"Hey, girls," a voice called out. "How're my faves doing?"

I didn't have to turn to see who it was. Nobody could mistake who that shrill tone belonged to. Since dying cats weren't a common occurrence at Bellamy, it could only be...

"Patti Lynn," I stated, rolling my eyes at Liza.

"The one and only," Patti replied, stepping to my side as if we invited her into our conversation. "But not the one and *lonely*."

Shocker. How did we know that was coming? Patti Lynn was one of those annoying students you wished you could hate but couldn't bring yourself to do it. She was loud, obnoxious, and somewhat nerdy, but didn't have a mean bone in her body. It made it difficult to send her away for fear she'd break down in tears and cause a scene in front of the entire school, making you feel like you were the worst person alive. She'd often go on and on about the latest fan fiction story she was writing and wouldn't let you get a word in until she was through describing the latest adventures of Rey, Han, Hermione, or whoever else occupied her fantasy world. Nobody here cared about her stories, but she wouldn't shut up long enough to let anyone tell her that. That's why it came as such a shock to everyone - her included - when two weeks earlier, she got asked out by Chris Green, president of the student council.

For the six months I'd known her, she'd shouted *"The one and only,"* whenever anyone called out her name. After Chris asked her out, she began adding, *"But not the one and lonely"* to her already irritating response. Liza and I didn't particularly like her, but we tolerated her.

"Hey, Patti," Liza greeted nonchalantly while muscling her locker shut.

"Hi," Patti returned, waving excitedly. "How many times have I told you girls to start calling me by my married name? It's Patti Green."

"Well, since you're not married..," I replied, grinning sarcastically and shrugging my shoulders.

"It's only a matter of time," she responded. "I'm sure Chris is planning to propose the day after we graduate."

Was it any wonder Chris was Patti's first boyfriend? So annoying.

"So, what you gals doing?" Patti persisted, believing the three of us were besties.

"You mean, besides being late for class?" Liza commented.

"I'll tell you what *I'm* doing," I said, plucking the lollipop from between my lips and pointing it at the huddled cheerleaders. "I'm going over there to talk with them."

"You're not serious," Liza griped.

"I am. I'm going to invite them to your party."

"I'm not having a party," Liza said.

Patti lit up excitedly, "You're having a party?" she questioned. "Can I come?"

"I'm not having a party!" Liza affirmed, more assertive that time.

"Whatever," I jumped in, "my point is, I'm going over there to talk with them."

I took a few steps toward the bleached bombshells, hearing Liza shout over my shoulder, "I'm not having a party."

I waved her comment off. "Relax."

I heard the two of them whispering their defiance behind my back, wondering if I would back down before confronting the popular cheer squad. If they knew me at all - truly knew who I was - it wouldn't have even been a question.

Sabrina, the tallest of the four, noticed me first, her lip curling into a sneer as I approached her teammate from behind. I understood her reaction. We'd had a bit of a.., I guess you could call it a rough start my first week here; I don't think she ever got over it. I wouldn't hold that against her. I'd probably give the same look if she tried encroaching on our space at Liza's locker. Who was I kidding? None of these girls would be caught dead fraternizing with our lowly kind. In their eyes, we weren't worthy enough to be occupying the same hallway as them. Yet, here I was, coming face to face with the enemy.

I lightly tapped the closest to me, Jill, on the shoulder to get her attention, hoping the touch of an inferior being wouldn't offend her.

"Jill, hi," I greeted, faking a smile, something for which I was an expert. "I'm Emma. We're in Human Physiology together."

"I know who you are," she returned snidely. "Can I help you?"

"I'm actually here on Liza's behalf; she was too embarrassed to come over here herself."

I watched all four girls' eyes shift over my shoulder in curiosity, a reaction I'd hoped for.

"It's kinda short notice, but she wanted to invite you to a party tonight."

"A party?" Jill questioned. "We're not going to that freak's house."

Sabrina took a hard look over my shoulder a second time, then back to her shorter teammate. "No way, isn't that right, girls?"

"That's right," responded one, while the other simply nodded.

"Oh, it's not at Liza's house," I responded. "It's at the old, abandoned mill. We're going to take over the entire second floor."

"That place is boarded up. You can't get in there."

"We already have. One of the windows wasn't sealed up. Anyway, it's already set to go. We've got music and alcohol. It's going to be a blast."

Jill looked me up and down, determining my character with only a glance at my appearance. I flashed an innocent smile. Appearances could be deceiving.

"Well, if it's at the old mill," Jill answered, looking at her squad mates, gleaning their acceptance, "I suppose we could make it."

"Great! It starts at seven o'clock. We'll see you there."

And with that, I turned away, now listening to *their* excited whispers as they dispersed to their classrooms.

"What did you say?" Liza asked upon my return, her face displaying annoyance.

"I invited them to your party."

"So, you *are* having a party," Patti said, clapping enthusiastically.

"No, I am most certainly not having a party," Liza replied. "How could you do that, Emma?"

"Didn't I tell you to relax?" I answered. "*We* know you're not having a party, but *they* don't. They're going to get quite the surprise when they show up at the old mill building tonight to find nobody there."

"You didn't!" Liza expressed.

"I did."

"So wait," Patti interjected. "You're *not* having a party?"

We both turned to her in unison and belted out, "There *is* no party."

Chapter 3

Hard Feelings

I didn't understand the cold shoulder Liza was giving me. I thought she'd find the prank amusing. She liked those four girls even less than I did. It wasn't that I was expecting adoration or applause, but friendly conversation during our study hall would have been a good start. Instead, she buried herself in her trigonometry book with only the occasional glance in my direction. Each time, I wanted to say, "Don't worry, I see you ignoring me," but that would have only made it worse. I opted to ride out the storm. She'd come around.

Speaking of coming around, I spied Patti sneaking through the doorway, inquisitively scanning for our location. I tried to duck my head into my book, but I wasn't fast enough. She caught a glimpse of me and speed-walked over.

"Well, to what do we owe this honor?" I questioned sarcastically.

Patti smiled from ear to ear. "Aww, that's so nice."

I don't think she understood sarcasm.

She plopped the soda bottle she'd been carrying onto the table and helped herself to a seat.

"Guys, I thought of a theme for the party tonight."

Liza tilted her book back to give Patti an evil stare over the top of it.

"I'm not having a party," she said through clenched teeth.

"Oh, but I thought..,"

"You thought wrong, Patti," I said.

She began nervously fidgeting, struggling to twist the cap off her bottle of generic brand cola.

"Well, I wasn't sure," she said. "Jill and the other girls were talking about it last period. They sounded pretty excited to be going."

"That's good," I responded. "The more excited they are, the more it works out in our favor."

"*Your* favor, you mean," Liza blurted. "I never wanted you to do that in the first place."

"Do what?" Patti asked, still fighting with her soda bottle. "I'm so confused."

"Oh my God, Patti!" I expressed. "How slow are you?"

"You don't have to be mean to her, Emma," Liza defended, though I knew it was only to show how upset she was with me. Then, she turned to Patti. "Patti, for the third time, there isn't a party tonight."

"Are you sure?" Patti asked, unwilling to accept the obvious.

"Yes, we're sure," I said, snatching the unopened bottle from Patti's hands after watching her fidget with the cap unsuccessfully for the last minute and a half. "It was just a prank."

I twisted the cap off and handed the bottle back to her. I'm sorry, but over a minute was all I could handle.

"Oh, Okay," Patti answered, taking a sip from her drink. "At least, Ricky will feel better about that."

"Ricky Meyers?" Liza questioned. "Why would *he* care?"

"Duh. Sabrina's boyfriend. I heard him tell Sabrina he didn't want her going because he had to work and didn't want her flirting with other guys."

"Not insecure or anything," I quipped.

Liza sat up. "I thought they broke up last month."

"No, they're still together," Patti replied. "I think he works a lot, though."

"So, you see," I stated, slapping my hand on the table. "We're actually doing a good thing by not having that party. We're keeping couples together in healthy relationships."

Liza gave me a side-eyed glare. "Not helping."

"Oh, come on," I said, playfully grinning. "That was funny. Don't be mad at me."

She shook her head and stared at the pages of her book. "I'm not mad at you," she said, exhaling heavily through her nose.

"Riiiight," I responded.

Then, there was silence for a moment before Patti spoke up.

"Don't be mad at me, either. It's like Chris says..," she reached up and pinched her cheeks. "I can't help being so darn cute."

Liza and I looked over at Patti and then at each other. Our blank stares only lasted a few seconds before we both erupted into laughter. Thanks, Patti. You managed to bring my friend back to me.

Chapter 4

Bad Behavior

I walked into the house to the sound of my mom's inharmonious laughter resonating from the other room. She was on the phone and hadn't heard me enter, as was evident by her jubilant tone. I overheard a portion of her conversation, which consisted of, "*Yes, I can't wait, either. It'll be fun.*" When I stepped into view, she flashed a nervous glare.

"Okay, you too," she quickly muttered. "Gotta go. Bye."

I gave her a questioning look. "What was that about?"

"Oh, nothing. Work."

"Work, huh?" I questioned.

"Yeah," she replied, then quickly changed the subject. "How was your day?"

Tell me that wasn't an obvious diversionary tactic. All right, Mom - I'll play along.

"It was fine. Liza got mad at me for a little while, but we worked things out."

"Why did she get mad at you?"

"Because I played a joke on those stupid cheerleaders I told you about."

"Emma!"

"Relax, Mom. It wasn't a big deal."

"Well, it must have been a big deal to Liza," she said. "And you didn't have to call those girls stupid."

Was she trying to make me feel bad?

"So, what was the joke that caused the hard feelings?" she questioned sternly. "And why did it bother Liza so much if it was about those other girls?"

"Because I told that cheerleader clique that Liza was throwing a party tonight at the old mill building."

"And I take it she's not?"

"Of course not."

"Emma, why would you do that?"

"It was harmless, Mom."

"Harmless or not, there was no reason for you to involve Liza in your little joke. I can see why she got upset. Did you, at least, tell those girls it wasn't Liza's idea when you explained to them you were only joking?"

"Ummm..,"

If it wasn't my grade school articulation that gave me away, I think it might have been my guilty expression.

"You *did* tell those girls, didn't you?" she questioned. I think she already knew the answer but wanted to hear from me.

"It's not a big deal, Mom. They'll get down there, see there's no party, and then go home."

"Emma, that's not the point. Are these the girls that gave you a hard time when we first arrived here? Jill, Sabrina, Beverly, and that other girl whose name I can never remember?"

"Trina," I jumped in. "That's them. Though it was only Sabrina who started trouble with me that first week."

"I remember. Either way, if they go down there only to find it was all just a silly prank, they're likely to take it out on Liza. I want you to call those girls and tell them it was a joke."

"What? No way, Mom. I can't do that now."

"And why not?"

"Listen, Mom, I know it's been forever since you were in high school, but once you set this kind of thing in motion, you gotta let it ride itself out. Besides, you don't know these girls. It will only make things worse if I tell them."

"Which is why you shouldn't have done it in the first place."

"They'll get over it."

"They *will* get over it," my mom responded, "because you're going to call them and call it off."

"I told you, I can't."

"You *can*, and you *will*."

"But, Mom..,"

"No 'buts,' Emma," she snapped back. "You call those girls and explain to them you were only joking. And you're going to apologize to them, too."

"Oh, no, I'm not." I huffed and stormed to the door.

"Where are you going?" my mom questioned.

"I'm going for a walk."

"I mean it," she responded. "I want you to call those girls."

"I'll text them on my walk," I said through gritted teeth.

"You'd better."

I wasn't texting them.

As I reached the door, my mom announced, "I won't be here when you get back. You'll have to make yourself dinner."

I turned, already upset, but now, more so.

"What? Where are you going?"

"I have to go into the office for a few hours. I have an important meeting."

"Right," I griped with cynicism. "Because that was 'work' that called you."

"That's right, it was."

"Oh, please."

"What's that supposed to mean?"

"A meeting, Mom? This late? I'm not a kid anymore. You don't have to hide that you're sleeping with Mr. Hendricks."

"What? Where did that come from?"

"I overheard you on the phone, Mom. *'You can't wait.' 'It'll be fun.'* That certainly doesn't sound work-related. He's a married man, Mom. You know things never work out well with married men."

"First of all, I'm not having an affair with Mr. Hendicks, and second, I don't appreciate you speaking to me that way."

"Whatever, Mom," I said heatedly, opening the door. "I guess I'm the only one in this house who always has to do the right thing."

I walked out and slammed the door behind me.

Chapter 5

Game Over

By 8:30 the next morning, between classes, an unhappy trio of hissing blondes stormed over to my locker, where Liza had accompanied me to investigate the myth about organizational skills among high school seniors. She tried warning me of the blonde brigade's impending arrival, but, in truth, I had plenty of time to prepare for the imminent approach the evening before after I got home from my walk. You can't swat at a bee's nest without expecting some of them to attack. And Jill, the queen bee of the foursome-minus-one, demanded it of her buzzing disciples.

"You must've thought that was really funny last night," Jill fumed, her cohorts Trina and Beverly nodding in agreement, their arms crossed about their B-cup chests while their tightly pulled ponytails wagged behind them.

"Whatever do you mean?" I questioned innocently, displaying a sarcastic, confused look.

"You know *exactly* what I'm talking about," she snarled. "The so-called party."

"Oh, yeah, right," I nodded. "It got canceled. Didn't you receive the message? I don't have many people's numbers, so I texted Mike and Sebastian about it."

I flashed Jill the same text message I used to appease my mom when she got back home from her little "meeting at work." Gross!

"I told those guys to let people know."

It's true; I did text the two football teammates the message. Not that it mattered. You see, I've somewhat mastered the art of listening to conversations that weren't necessarily intended for my ears. That's how I've learned many of the secrets I've kept locked away, only to be pulled out and dusted off in times of need. The key is to make note of the phone numbers you gather without alerting those who wouldn't otherwise willingly share that information with you. It's not my fault if neither Mike nor Sebastian has my number programmed into their phones, therefore having no inkling as to who the text message was from or, since there was never a party to begin with, what it was about. And if Jill or her lackeys confronted them, they had the text message to prove I wasn't lying.

"That's so frustrating they didn't tell you," I added, looking the part. "I hope you didn't go all that way only to find the building boarded up."

"Ha ha," Jill said with a sneer. "I bet that was your intention all along."

"It wasn't," I replied. "I'm truly sorry if it caused you any inconvenience."

"Whatever," Jill hissed. "I should have known better than to trust you freaks. I was only going so I could rub it in your face when nobody showed up to your stupid, loser party, anyhow. Come on, girls."

She walked away feeling triumphant, followed by her dimwitted compatriots.

"You know," Liza began in a hushed tone, "it's probably not the smartest idea to get on those girls' bad side."

"Who cares?" I responded. "They're just a bunch of stuck-up snots who think they're better than everyone else. I think deep down, they probably hate themselves."

"Don't hold back," Liza said, grinning. "Tell me how you *really* feel."

"Let's go," I said, shaking my head and snatching my English Literature book from my locker. "We're going to be late to class."

It was during Study Hall, at around 11:15, when Liza and I first heard the whispered threads of the rampant rumor mill that was the Bellamy student body. The ever-jovial Patti seized the opportunity to interrupt my attempt at dozing off while staring down my calculus homework. Liza was on her phone, paying little attention to my occasional head bobs as I tried desperately to keep my forehead from hitting the pages of my book. Patti clopped her way over like a proud Clydesdale and sank into a chair beside me.

"Did you hear the latest, guys?" she asked, twisting the cap off her bottle of cola.

Now wide awake, I sprang at the opportunity.

"You found out you're the illegitimate love child of Mr. Hopper," I said excitedly.

"The Phys Ed teacher?" she questioned. "Ew. No. My dad is Daniel Lynn."

Clearly, playful jibes and subtle mockery were not Patti's strong suit.

Realizing Patti's shortcomings, Liza jumped in. "I think what Emma meant to say was, 'We give up.'"

"Oh. Well, I overheard a couple of the girls talking in the hall," Patti replied. "Apparently, Jill was on the phone getting grilled by Sabrina's mother because Sabrina never made it home after the party last night."

"There *was* no party," Liza responded, rolling her eyes.

"That's what I thought," Patti returned. "But I heard them say they were all together at the old mill last night. I assumed that meant you guys ended up having the party after all."

"Well, we didn't," I said. "That's the whole point of a prank."

"Whatever it was," Patti continued, "it ended with Sabrina going missing."

"Wait, what?" Liza said, sitting up in her chair, suddenly interested in Patti's words. "Jill and the other cheerleaders don't know where she is?"

"They said they haven't heard from her," Patti replied, shaking her head.

"She probably just met up with her boyfriend and stayed out with him all night," I stated, watching Patti guzzle down half of the 20 oz bottle of liquid caffeine and sugar.

"I don't know," she replied, wiping her sleeve across her lips. "I saw her boyfriend Ricky in third-period chemistry. You'd think Sabrina would be in school, too. Anyway, I hope it's nothing too serious." She stood up and polished off the last of her soft drink. "I gotta get back to the AV room before Mrs. Donaldson realizes I'm not there." She started walking away, then stopped and turned to us. "I'm glad you guys didn't have the party without me." She flashed us a grin that made you want to get up and hug her. We didn't. But I'd be lying if I said I wasn't tempted.

"Don't you think that's weird?" Liza questioned.

"I know," I returned. "She drank the entire bottle in less than thirty seconds."

"Not that," Liza said. "I'm talking about Sabrina not making it home last night."

"I don't know if it's weird," I replied. "Haven't you ever stayed out all night?"

"Yeah, of course, but I have a good reason to. The longer I'm away from my mom, the better. Plus, my friends always know where I am."

"What friends?" I said jokingly.

"Funny." She gave me a scathing look. "I'm serious, though. Doesn't it seem unusual that Sabrina wouldn't just go home like the other three girls?"

I nodded. "Yeah, I suppose. But why are you so concerned about it? Those girls have never done anything nice to have someone worrying over them."

I noticed Liza's expression sour.

"You haven't known them as long as I have."

It was true. Six months was not a long time to get to know someone. But I knew of their kind. And I knew what Sabrina did to me my first week at Bellamy. Still, Liza had known those girls since middle school. I'm sure there were a few decent times in all those years.

"Listen, I'm sure it's nothing. But if it *is* something, well, like Patti said, let's hope it's nothing serious."

Chapter 6

School Daze

The school day progressed as usual. In between classes, students wandered the halls, demonstrating their best impersonations of zombies. I wasn't too far behind the unenthusiastic walking dead. The good news was that I only had one class left to make it through - then I could go home and crash for an hour or two before dinner. Unfortunately, that one class was physics, the subject I had muddled through all year. I wasn't built for it. Why should I care that the laws of physics dictate a bumblebee can't fly yet somehow does? That sounds stupid. Did they ever think maybe the laws were wrong? Could we even trust that Newton guy? I certainly didn't know him. In fact, the only Newton I ever liked was the fig variety. Wait, that's not true. I wanted to be Olivia Newton-John for like two years after the first time I saw her in Grease. And no matter what I did, I couldn't convince my mom to buy me a pair of those leather pants she wore in the movie or let me dye my hair blonde, so that sucked. But also, come to think of it, my mom got me into *Wayne* Newton for a spell. She liked him when she was a young girl, and as a result, used to play his CDs all the time while cooking dinner. It ruined me. How many times can you listen to Danke Shoen before you want to throw yourself off a bridge? If you're keeping score, the answer is seventy-two. I far surpassed that number by the time I was eight. The only reason I'm still among the living is because my town didn't have any bridges tall enough to cause any more damage than a sprained ankle. Maybe that was a blessing in disguise. Being stuck at home with an injured leg would mean more Danke Shoen. No thanks.

Lucky for me, my daydreaming got me through another yawn-inducing physics lesson without Mr. Hanson noticing the glossy film over my eyes. When the final bell sounded, a thunderous eruption of chair legs slid out from under desks, shattering decibel records previously set by Air Force pilots. Students flooded into the hallway in a mass exodus from their respective classrooms. I was caught in the current, sandwiched between Lyle Kermuckle, who didn't believe in using deodorant, and Amy Fister, one-half of the acne twins who, along with her sister Carol, had enough zits to give even Dr. Pimple Popper nightmares. One misstep on my part, and I ran the risk of either being smothered in rancid underarm sweat or popping a goo-filled projectile. The odds weren't in my favor, but I'd escaped worse situations unscathed. I could do it again.

Once out in the hall, I glimpsed Patti weaving her way around the mob of anxious departers, making a beeline toward me. I tried avoiding her by turning in the opposite direction, hoping she hadn't seen me, but I was fighting a losing battle against the tide. She caught up to me before I could make it to the gymnasium, where I had planned to duck out the back door, never to be seen again. Well, not until the next day, anyway.

"Emma, wait up," she cried, sounding so desperately like she needed a friend. I felt my shoulders drop. I couldn't help myself. How could I refuse such neediness?

"Patti," I acknowledged, halting my progress to let her catch up.

"The one and…"

"Yeah, yeah," I interrupted. "I get it. You're not lonely. What's up? I'm kind of in a rush."

"I was just wondering if Liza was all right."

"What do you mean?" I asked.

"She took off before the last period started. She grabbed her things and walked out, looking pretty upset."

I shook my head, trying to recall if Liza had mentioned something to me that I perhaps forgot.

"No," I replied. "Before the last period started? Huh. I don't know what that was about. Maybe *her* period started, and she didn't have any tampons."

"Oh, well, I just thought you would have known. You know, since you're seeing each other."

"What?" I questioned loudly, taken aback by Patti's comment. "We're not seeing each other. Why the hell would you think that?"

Admittedly, I was a little annoyed.

"Well, you two are always so close. Plus, I overheard Jill tell Sebastian that she caught you two making out in the bathroom."

"She said that?" I said through clenched teeth, fuming.

"Yeah. Earlier today in biology."

"I don't believe this! That little bleach-headed bitch! Wait until I get my hands on her."

"Do you think that had something to do with why Liza left?" Patti questioned.

"No way," I replied. "Liza couldn't care less what any of those cheerleading ass-clowns think of her. I mean, I don't either, but I'm not going to let that fake skank get away with spreading lies about us."

"Okay, but really?" Patti said, looking skeptical. "You and Liza *aren't* dating? It's okay if you are. Even if only to make someone else jealous."

"Jealous? Oh my God, Patti," I shouted, rolling my eyes. "I'm not gay."

"Sorry," Patti said, frantically waving her hands in front of her chest as if she thought I was going to haul off and belt her. "I didn't know."

"Whatever," I responded. "I gotta go."

I walked away, knowing Patti's frowning face was gnawing at my back. I felt bad leaving her like that, but I didn't have the patience for her obnoxious naivety. Instead, my concern quickly shifted to Liza's sudden, unexpected departure. I wondered what could have caused her to leave without even texting me. Whatever it was, I wasn't about to ignore what could be a cry for help. I pulled my cell phone from my back pocket and began texting.

```
Hey, I missed you after class today. Where
were you? You could have saved me from Pat-
ti's non-stop ridiculous blathering.
```

There. That'd do it. It was just enough to get a response without letting her know I was worried. Did I mean that? Was I worried? I hadn't thought about it before. I guess I was - in a purely selfish way. Without Liza in school, I'd have to deal with Patti's incessant babbling on my own. If that were to happen..? My one saving grace was that *this* town had taller bridges.

Chapter 7

Better Left Unsaid

My house was only a little over a mile from the school, so it didn't take me long to walk home. Still, I thought I would have heard back from Liza within the first quarter mile. That didn't happen. Instead, I'd texted three times since, and she hadn't responded to any of them. Now, granted, it's only been an hour and a half since I left school, but come on. A girl can't wait all night.

From my bedroom, I heard the front door open and close. Seconds later, my mom's voice cried out, summoning me from the comfort of my bed and saving my poor thumbs from cramping by the constant, mundane scrolling through Instagram posts.

"Emma? Are you home?"

"Yeah," I replied through the cheap, hollow bedroom door as I slid myself off the side of the mattress.

"Can you come down here for a moment?" she requested. "I want to talk to you about something."

"I'm coming," I replied.

Here's the thing – if you knew my mom at all, you'd have thought that was weird. Don't get me wrong; we communicated all the time, but it was usually through natural conversations that came up when we were in the same room together. She never forced a conversation upon me. The fact that she disturbed me from my mind-numbing social media surfing was unheard of. She was probably desperate to apologize to me for the way she handled things last night. I suppose I could do a little apologizing of my own.

I exited my room and sluggishly made my way down the stairs. My mom was waiting for me in the foyer.

"Hey, Mom," I greeted, sitting down on the second step from the bottom. "What's up?"

She flashed me a half-hearted smile as if unsure she was ready to commit to the conversation she initiated. I stared uncomfortably at her, shifting my eyes several times to the side, then back to her. She got the hint.

"I don't want you to freak out," she began, running her fingers through her hair and twirling the ends around her index finger – something she always did when she was nervous. I think it might have been those same nerves that caused the prominent streak of gray hair along the left side of her head. "There may be a surprise tomorrow when you get home from school."

She gave me a hopeful glance as she bit down on the right side of her bottom lip.

"What is it?" I asked, wondering where this was coming from. She didn't make a habit of apologizing with bribery. I didn't recall asking for anything, and my birthday was still six months away. "And why are you acting nervous?"

"I'm not nervous." She responded by immediately dropping her hand from her hair-twirling fidgetiness. "And I can't tell you; otherwise, it'll ruin the surprise."

"Then why tell me at all?" I questioned.

"I guess I was a little excited and wanted to share my excitement with my wonderful daughter. Is that so bad?"

I gave her a questionable glare. "Wonderful daughter?" I responded quizzically. "You're being weird."

"I'm not being weird," she said with a slight giggle as she went back to twirling her hair. "You *are* a wonderful daughter, and I think you should hear it more."

"First of all," I started while grinning, "I *know* I'm a wonderful daughter. Duh. No reminder needed. And second, you can't call me down here, start speaking about a surprise, and then leave me hanging like that. Can't you give me a little hint about what it is?"

"Nope," she said, leaning forward and lightly tapping her finger on the tip of my nose like she did when I was seven. "Because then it might not happen. Plus, I didn't want to miss that wonderfully annoyed look on your face." Then, she smirked and walked away toward the kitchen.

She could kiss my apology goodbye, then.

"But Mom..," I squeaked out before my vibrating pocket captured my attention.

I pulled my phone out and stared at the words on the screen. I felt my chest tighten.

"I hope you're hungry," my mother called out from the kitchen. "I'm making chicken alfredo for dinner."

I glanced toward the kitchen, then back to my phone, my heart pounding a mile a minute.

"Mom, I can't," I yelled. "I gotta go."

I quickly strode to the front door as my mother breached the kitchen doorway.

"But it's your favorite. Where are you going?"

In my head, I was already gone. I closed the door behind me without a response. What was I supposed to say? *Sorry, Mom, something came up; I can't stay.* She'd expect an explanation. That was something I couldn't give. I peered back at my phone as I headed down the street, the text message blatantly taunting me.

`Did you think you'd get away with it?`

Chapter 8

More than Serious

I kept telling myself, *Today was a new day.* I didn't know what that was last night, receiving a random text from an unknown number that caused me to panic. I had to get out of the house to get some air – to clear my head. But for what reason? The text didn't mean anything. It couldn't. The more I thought about it, the more I believed it was meant for someone else. The sender had the wrong number, that's all. It had to be. But now I knew how confused Mike and Sebastian must have been when they received *my* text the other day.

I brushed off the anxiety after a long walk around the block and several more texts to Liza, which all went unanswered. The good news was, with the worries of my own situation swirling around my brain, my concern over Liza's lack of

41

response was less traumatizing to my ego. I rationalized the silence as only Liza's irresponsibility of not charging her phone before it died. It wasn't the first time it'd happened. It probably wouldn't be the last. I could have called her to confirm, but Liza didn't like talking on the phone, and I didn't want to chance upsetting her.

My mom was a touch disappointed in me when I returned an hour later from my reflective jaunt. I didn't understand her reasoning. Dinner wasn't even ready yet when I got back home. She said she was worried about me, the way I just walked out, but she didn't press the subject. I appreciated that she respected my privacy. I didn't want to lie to her. Again.

Now, I reminded myself, yet again, as I strolled down the hallway on my way to homeroom, *Today was a new day.* As I passed by the "popular girl's club," it didn't escape my notice that Sabrina was still absent from their ranks. It was clear *I* hadn't escaped *their* notice either, as the heat from their sneers and hellfire glares burned into me like a sun. Ordinarily, I would have laughed it off and smiled at them, but this being the second day of Sabrina's mysterious absence, it didn't feel appropriate. I averted my eyes instead.

Stepping into homeroom, my eyes immediately scanned those present until they landed on Liza, who acknowledged me with a subtle head nod. She was sitting down, watching me traverse the maze of desks on my way to my chair beside hers. She didn't display a hint of guilt for ignoring my texts, which I thought she would. It didn't matter; I was already over it. I was relieved to see her, though.

"Did you get around to charging your phone?" I asked. I stood beside my desk while leaning my butt against its top edge.

"What do you mean?" Liza asked.

"Last night," I replied. "When you didn't respond to my texts, I assumed your phone had died."

"No, I saw your texts," she responded. "I was busy with something."

I felt a twinge of anger. All those hours I spent worrying, thinking Liza might need my help with something or maybe someone to talk to, was all for nothing. She ghosted me. Okay, maybe I wasn't over it after all. Now I was angry. But I had to watch myself. I didn't like people knowing my emotions.

"Oh," was all I mustered as I watched her nervously rolling her pen between her thumb and forefinger. I was trying so hard not to let her see the frustration oozing from me, but watching her fiddle with that damn pen and knowing she ignored me was testing my tolerance.

"Miss Murphy," our homeroom teacher, Mr. Dodd, announced as he entered the classroom, "will you kindly take your seat?"

Saved by the teacher.

Behind me, Brett Blevins, who fancied himself the class clown, shouted, "Where would you like her to take it?" It garnered only a few chuckles.

"Very funny, Mr. Blevins," Mr. Dodd replied, placing his leather portfolio on his desk. "It's good to hear some of the same jokes that were old when I was your age are still prevalent today. The classics never die, do they?"

"Apparently not," Brett responded. "*You're* still with us."

That remark attracted more student responses than the previous one – only with moans instead of laughter. And, though Mr. Dodd *was* in his late sixties and probably should have retired years earlier, that comment was a little harsh and took things a bit too far. Even so, the elderly teacher brushed it off like a champ.

"I'll take that as a compliment, Mr. Blevins. I've always regarded myself as a classic kind of guy. Now, if you'll all settle down while I take attendance, I won't have to hold any of you back when the first bell rings."

Mr. Dodd dutifully marked his attendance book while I continued to stare at Liza fiddling with her pen, her eyes trained forward but her mind somewhere distant.

"Earth to Liza," I whispered. "Is everything..."

"Sabrina is still missing," Liza fired back. "Nobody's heard from her. I told you not to say anything about a party. Why did you do that?"

"Ladies," Mr. Dodd called out. "Is there a reason I'm still hearing your voices after I requested everyone to quiet down?"

"Actually, Mr. Dodd," Brett spoke out again, unable to contain himself, "you said '*settle* down,' not '*quiet* down.'"

I think Mr. Dodd had had enough and was about to lay the hammer down when Liza suddenly jumped from her seat and stormed out of the classroom.

"Liza!" I yelled, but she was oblivious to my cry. I didn't go after her; I didn't think she'd want me to. Instead, I stared at the pen she'd left behind on her desk, wondering what had happened.

She didn't leave school as she had done the day before, but she did her best to avoid me most of the day. I thought I'd reach out to her after lunch to find out what was going on, but instead, I learned in the worst way imaginable.

We all did.

At around 1:35, we found out just how serious things had become when an officer showed up to deliver the bad news to Principal Malik. Sabrina was no longer missing. Instead, her body had been found at the old mill building. The word "murder" rolled off people's tongues in whispers and hushed murmurings, spreading like a contagious virus throughout the school. Nobody knew what had happened for sure, but one thing was certain.

Sabrina was dead.

Chapter 9
Don't

An impromptu assembly was called to share the devastating news with the students. Guidance Councilor Davis opened his office as a sort of triage for those who needed to let their anger and frustration out. I wasn't one of them. It's not that I didn't care about Sabrina's death, but I had been through all this before when authorities discovered Mr. Blouth's half-eaten body in the forest back home. *He* was someone I liked. I didn't know Sabrina well enough to have such feelings.

I wasn't the only student failing to convey my emotionally stricken teenage angst, but I never expected Liza to break down as she had. I walked in on her in the bathroom, her body crouched in a ball on the floor, streaks of black mascara running down her cheeks, displaying the history of her pain and sorrow. I tried to console her, but she threw her hand forward and shoved me back.

"Don't," she said through quivering lips.

"What's going on Liza?" I asked. "I'm only trying to be your friend. We're all hurt by Sabrina's death, but you've been acting strange for the past couple of days. Talk to me. I'm right here."

"You don't get it, do you?" Liza said.

"Get what? That a classmate is dead? Of course, I do, and it sucks. But I don't understand why you're getting so emotional about it. You didn't even like her."

"Oh my God, Emma!" Liza blurted. "You're such an idiot sometimes! We were seeing each other!"

I stumbled back a step and felt my jaw almost hit the floor. It wasn't a reaction I was used to.

You had to understand; I was the girl who always knew everyone's secret, yet there I was, completely stupefied by what I'd just learned. Liza had shared with me all the nasty things she'd been through with her mother, the school, the students, and their parents but never once confided in me about her relationship with Sabrina. And worse, I never caught on to their secret.

"Y-you were?" I stuttered. "But Ricky..? Oh shit! I didn't know."

"Nobody knew," Liza responded. "That was the point. Sabrina didn't want anyone to know she was gay. Can you imagine how that would have played out with all her uppity friends - especially if they found out she was dating *me*? That's all they would have concerned themselves with, someone like me tarnishing their perfect images."

"But why didn't you tell *me*?" I asked, still processing how I could have missed the signs.

"I promised her I wouldn't say anything.., to anybody. I loved her so much; I didn't want to risk losing her."

"Liza, I..,"

I took a step forward, then paused, recalling the shove she gave me moments earlier.

"I'm so sorry," I continued, holding firm several feet away. "I don't know what to say. I want to hug you, take away your pain, do something, but I know it will never be enough."

"Haven't you done enough already?" Liza replied through clenched teeth. "It was your stupid prank that caused this. She never would have gone to that building if it wasn't for you."

"That's not fair. I didn't mean for anything bad to happen. It was only a joke."

"Yeah, well, your joke got my girlfriend killed."

More dark tears streamed from her eyes. She wiped her face with her sleeve, staining the fabric with damp blotches of black makeup. She glared at me with such disdain. She blamed me. At the moment, she *hated* me. I had to do something to change that. It wasn't right. I had to figure this out. I could get over others' negative feelings toward me, but I couldn't handle Liza not liking me.

Just then, the door flew open, and Mrs. Galviston, the principal's administrative assistant, barged in, interrupting my thoughts.

"Oh, *there* you are, Emma," she announced before noticing Liza crumpled up against the wall. "Is everything all right, girls?" she questioned. She gave me a suspicious glare as if I had done something to put Liza in her current position.

Liza looked up but remained silent. I jumped in to mitigate Mrs. Galviston's misgivings of our awkward appearance.

"Liza's taking Sabrina's death pretty hard. They were good friends."

"Oh no," the secretary said, her face showing remorse. "I know this is an awful situation. Should we call your mother to..,"

"NO!" Liza shouted over the woman.

Mrs. Galviston glanced at me; I offered a subtle shake of my head.

"All right then," the administrative assistant continued. "But we can't have you hanging out in the bathroom now, can we? Miss Faraday, I think it would do you some good to schedule an appointment with Guidance Counselor Davis. Talking about these things can help. Sometimes, we need to let our anger out to begin the process of healing."

"We were just discussing that, Mrs. Galviston," I responded. "Thank you."

"Very good," she replied. "As for you, Miss Murphy, you're presence is requested in the principal's office."

"Me?" I questioned.

"Is there another Emma Murphy in here?" she replied.

I glanced back at Liza, her hateful stare replaced with curiosity. I shrugged my shoulders, pretending she cared.

"Okay," I said. "Principal's office it is."

Chapter 10
School of Hard Knox

Mrs. Galviston led me down the hall to Principal Malik's office, keeping a watchful eye on me as if I didn't know where I was going or maybe thinking I would suddenly take off. Why would I do that? Principal Malik was a cool guy, and I could tell he liked me from the moment I stepped foot in the building all those months ago. That was when I knew things would be just like back home.

Well, maybe not *just* like back home.

I entered the small waiting area just outside Principal Malik's office, and my eyes immediately latched onto Patti sitting in one of the four wooden chairs that rested along the two side walls. Her expression was defeated and gloomy, a look I hadn't seen before from her normally cheery demeanor, and it only slightly brightened when she noticed my entrance.

"Sit there, please," Mrs. Galviston said, pointing to a chair along the opposite wall from where Patti sat. "I'll let them know you're both here."

She walked by me to notify the principal while I looked over at Patti, curiously questioning the assistant's use of pronouns by exaggeratingly but silently mouthing the word '*them*?' to Patti. Patti tilted her head sideways and shrugged. I never perceived Principal Malik as a they/them kind of guy, thinking he was too "old school" to prescribe to such modern thought. Good for him.

It was only when Mrs. Galviston opened the principal's door that I glimpsed the reasoning behind her curious use of "them" and why my breathing suddenly became shallower.

I noticed two men standing with Principal Malik: one a uniformed officer and the other casually dressed in jeans and a dark brown sweater, the collar of his light blue button-up shirt protruding from the sweater's neckline. His sandy brown hair was slicked back, molded perfectly to his scalp, and held in place by gel. He wasn't bad looking for an older man - maybe in his late twenties. The officer was more ragged-looking with his dark complexion and pock-marked cheeks. His unattractive features became more noticeable when he saw me staring through the narrow opening and shot me an unpleasant glare. Or was that his natural look? It was hard to say.

I suddenly became nervous, though I didn't know why. I felt my legs begin to shake uncontrollably. To disguise their involuntary motion, I began to slide my fingers back and forth along my thighs.

"Patti," Mrs. Galviston said, pulling her head from the open door.

Like a reflex, Patti's chin shot upward as she erupted, "The one and.., oh," then silenced herself, tucking her chin to her chest.

"They'd like to speak with you first," Mrs. Galviston continued, unfazed by Patti's outburst.

Patti didn't initially get up but instead curled her hand inward, pointing to herself like she thought perhaps the secretary had misspoken and meant to call *me* first. Mrs. Galviston raised her left eyebrow and nodded. I watched Patti's shoulders drop like bricks as she stood and slowly shuffled forward, glancing back at me with a pouty face as she slid between the principal's assistant and the open door. After Patti crossed the entrance's threshold into the seemingly terrifying unknown, Mrs. Galviston softly closed the door behind her.

"So what's that all about?" I questioned, lifting my hand from my lap just high enough to point unenthusiastically.

The woman's eyes narrowed, keen to my feeble attempt at siphoning information.

"You'll get your chance soon enough when they call you in," she replied.

You couldn't blame me for trying. At my last school, it worked like a charm. These people had yet to warm up to me. They would. I just needed to give them more time. In my present situation, time was something I had in abundance as I nervously twiddled my thumbs, wondering what was happening beyond that door. Since a police officer was here, I imagined it had something to do with Sabrina's death, though I wondered why Patti and I were requested to speak with him. And why separately? As Mrs. Galviston stated, I'm sure I'd learn soon enough.

With each passing second, my confidence was shrinking and my anxiety rising. *'Soon enough'* turned into thirty-five grueling minutes, during which time I couldn't keep my legs from bouncing, and I gnawed four fingernails to extinction before starting on the skin around my fingertips. My mom's going to be pissed when I tell her I'm not hungry for dinner tonight because I practically ate my hand - unless it's roast pork and sauerkraut. There's always room for that. Maybe if I kept thinking about food, my thoughts would settle down. But that wasn't to be.

At the first rattling of the door knob, I abruptly sat up in my chair to give the appearance that I wasn't nervous. *Was* I nervous? Wait, let my fingernails answer that. But why? For what reason would I need to be worried?

The answer came to me seconds later when Patti exited the principal's office with her eyes focused on the ground. She slowly walked by me with her arms crossed about her chest like she was hugging herself for moral support, ignoring that I was even in the room. When she reached the far door and was about to leave, she stopped, looked over her shoulder with her eyes still trained downward, and whispered, "I'm so sorry, Emma," then walked out.

If I wasn't nervous before, that did the trick. There was no way I could pretend I was keeping it together after that.

"Emma," Principal Malik's voice rang out. "We'll see you now."

Chapter 11

When Will You Learn

I noticed that the officer remained standing as I took my seat across from Principal Malik, even though there was a vacant chair to my left. To my right sat the good-looking man with the slicked-back hair. Now that I was closer and got a better look at him, his skin was so smooth, and his smile inviting, with a hint of his sparkling white teeth showing through the slight gap between his perfectly shaped lips. The sound of Bon Jovi's Bed of Roses began playing in the background as the handsome man winked at me, a magical twinkle in his..,

"Miss Murphy!" Principal Malik snapped, the sound of a needle scratching off a vinyl record awakening me from my daydream.

I turned and looked at the principal in confusion, wanting to go back to that other place in my head - angry that they took me out of it and maybe a little embarrassed.

"Detective Harrison asked you a question," he continued.

"What? Oh," was all I managed to squeak out.

Good one, Emma. Way to act natural. Did he say 'detective'? The guy's a detective? I looked back at the man sitting beside me. He was stone-faced and no longer the man I thought I wanted to spend the rest of my life with. *You cut me deep*, I thought. *You had me fooled with your finely sculpted hair and chiseled cheekbones. Well played, sir; well played.*

"Can you repeat the question, please?" I asked, ignoring the standing officer's frustrated huff.

"I asked if you could tell me the last time you saw your classmate, Sabrina Beaulieu."

"Um, two days ago. Wednesday."

He scribbled my answers on a notepad resting on his lap.

"And where was that?"

"Here at school."

"Did you see her after school?"

"No," I answered. "We don't really hang out."

The detective looked up from his pad, "And yet you invited her to a party," he stated, skeptical of my previous answer.

I tried so hard not to roll my eyes. "There wasn't a party."

"But your friend, Patti," he pointed his pen toward the closed door, "she told us you were having a party that night and that you invited Sabrina and some other girls."

I let out an audible gasp as I shook my head.

"There wasn't a party," I repeated. "It was a joke."

"A joke?" Principal Malik spoke up.

"You know, a prank," I stated, turning to see the disappointment on his face, something I hadn't seen from him before.

"A prank that ended in a student's death," Detective Harrison stated, applying a dash of salt to the slowly opening wound.

"How was I supposed to know those girls would take me seriously? They don't even like me."

"I see," the detective said. "And by 'those girls,'" he flipped up the top page of his pad to read from the page below, "you're referring to Jill Wells, Trina Sapply, and Beverly Peentu?"

"Yes."

"Okay," he said, nodding and biting his lower lip. "Can you tell us where you were that night?"

"Home."

"You were home the entire night?" he questioned.

I suddenly thought about the argument I'd gotten into with my mom and how I left the house for a while. If only I'd listened to her and called those girls to cancel the party. My knee started bobbing.

"I left for a little while to go for a walk."

"A walk to the old mill building, perhaps?"

"No," I said angrily. "I went around the block."

"Okay," he responded, his face displaying doubt. He leaned sideways and reached down into a leather bag beside his chair. He pulled out a large, ziplocked freezer bag and held it up for me. Inside the clear plastic was an empty soda bottle.

"Do you recognize this?" the detective asked.

I flashed a quizzical look, "It's a soda bottle."

"It's a soda bottle that was left at the crime scene," he said, "only a few feet from Sabrina's body."

"Okay," I responded. "So what? I don't drink soda."

"Then, can you explain how your fingerprints are all over this one?"

"What? No, I..,"

My mind jolted back to a year earlier when I was fingerprinted as part of a CORI background check as a requirement to help assist at an after-school program at Gibson Elementary. I only agreed because it was Mr. Blouth who asked. And my prints were supposed to be removed after six months. That clearly didn't happen. Great system they've got there. Son of a..,

Then my thoughts flashed to yesterday when I impatiently grabbed Patti's bottle and helped her remove the cap. That was the same bottle.

"That must be Patti's soda," I spoke up. "She had it with her during Study Hall the other day but couldn't get the cap off, so I helped her with it. *Her* fingerprints must be on it, too."

"Oh, they are," the detective said. "And she corroborated what you just told us. But here's the thing," he continued, "we're wondering how it ended up at the crime scene - and with no other prints on it. Patti has an alibi for where she was that evening. She was working with Mrs. Donaldson in the AV Department, getting things set up for the upcoming graduation ceremony. Mrs. Donaldson already confirmed as much. You, on the other hand, went 'for a walk.'"

I didn't appreciate that he used his fingers as air quotes when he said that, as if he didn't believe me.

"You think I had something to do with Sabrina's death?" I questioned heatedly. "I didn't."

"I never said you did, Miss Murphy," the detective replied. "I merely repeated what you had already stated."

"Well, shouldn't I have my mom here or a lawyer or something?" I looked to Principal Malik for guidance.

"Oh, you're not in any trouble, Emma," he assured me. "These officers are simply here to ask questions."

"That's right, Miss Murphy," the detective added. "Nobody is being accused of anything. We're only gathering information to determine the events leading up to Miss Beaulieu's death. We'll be meeting with other students as well."

"In that case, I've told you everything I know - which is nothing. So, can I go now?"

I noticed Principal Malik glance at the detective, asking for approval. Detective Harrison nodded.

"Thank you, Emma," the principal said. "You can go now."

I didn't hesitate; I jumped from my seat. As I started for the door, the detective made a final comment.

"Thank you for your cooperation, Miss Murphy."

I didn't say anything back, only nodding my response. As I walked out of the office and out of the waiting area, I kept thinking two things: How could Patti rat me out about the party like that, and strangely, why were *Patti's* fingerprints already in the police database?

Chapter 12

Patti's Story

On my walk home, I couldn't get it out of my head. Were the police questioning students to get the full picture of events before Sabrina's death, as Detective Harrison had mentioned, or did they really think I had something to do with it? They couldn't possibly think that, could they? They had an empty soda bottle with my fingerprints on it. That didn't mean anything. I'm not a detective, but even I knew a crime scene could be manipulated to look like something it wasn't. How easy would it be for someone wearing gloves to plant a piece of incriminating evidence? Detective Harrison knew that, too, but he wanted to hear what we had to say. If either of us lied or tripped up, we'd look suspicious. In that respect, I couldn't blame Patti for spilling the beans about the party that never happened. It was the *other* thing I was more curious about. We were both called into the principal's office for questioning. The police had my prints in their system, illegally, mind you, because of a CORI check, but what about Patti's prints?

You have to understand - I'm very serious about secrets: learning them, keeping them, and using them, should the need arise. It can be frustrating to discover others' secrets have been kept from *me*. I've learned of two today: first, Liza's, and now Patti's. That didn't make me happy. How did I not know these things? Was I losing my touch?

I liked learning people's secrets firsthand. I'd get to know them, chat about my childhood, and let them slowly open up about who they were. I'd dig a little; they'd share a little more. I'd tug on their heartstrings; they'd let more slip. It was a process. If that didn't work, I'd do it the old-fashioned way: Google them. With Patti, I thought I knew it all, but now, it seemed, there was more to learn. Someone wasn't playing the game fairly.

Patti was adopted by Daniel and Linda Lynn when she was thirteen months old. Daniel and Linda's first daughter, Kelly, died in childbirth due to complications during the delivery. After that, Linda was unable to bear children.

Growing up in the Lynn household was a blessing for Patti. Her parents spoiled her rotten.

But it was rough, too. When she was seven years old, she broke her arm while trying to climb a tree in her backyard. After having lost one child and then having another injure herself, the Lynns became very protective of their daughter. She was no longer allowed outside without supervision.

As an only child with overly protective parents, Patti had only herself to play with. She said she would spend hours in her room, drawing and writing about all the characters she loved from her favorite movies and books. In elementary school, she avoided becoming friends with the other students since her parents wouldn't allow her to attend their birthday parties or even play with them after school.

On her eleventh birthday, at the risk of hurting their daughter, Patti's parents decided it was time to tell her she was adopted. After many questions and talking it through, it made Patti more appreciative of their love. After all, they could have chosen any child, but they chose *her*.

Her parents also told her about her stillborn sister, Kelly. Patti said, after that, she understood why her parents kept her so close and that that made her get even closer with them.

By the time Patti entered high school, she'd already been labeled a "weirdo" and "freak" by her peers. They'd never gotten the chance to know her. Not really. And it certainly didn't help that her obsessive blathering about fictional characters, whom someone her age should have abandoned years earlier, only compounded the issue. Her peppy and cheery (and, at times, naïve) attitude should have gained her friends but instead, came across as annoying and insincere. She was too needy and immature.

Even over time, the other students still couldn't bring themselves to like her. They merely tolerated her in small doses.

And that, in a nutshell, was Patti's life.

I weaved through the memories of the conversations I'd had with her, the things I'd learned from other students' whispers. She'd been a homebody her entire life, watched over by her parents. She never went out with others, never dated anyone before Chris Green asked her out, and didn't have a job. She didn't go to parties and wasn't a member of any school clubs. She hadn't participated in anything that required a background check. What was I missing? What did she do to have her fingerprints in the national database? It was bugging me almost as much as Detective Harrison's unbelieving stare, but it would have to take a backseat.

As I turned the corner onto my street, I noticed an unfamiliar car, an old one at that, parked in our driveway. My mom's voice echoed in my head.

"There may be a surprise tomorrow when you get home from school."

Great! Fantastic! That's just what I needed. Unless that car was a gift for me, which I highly doubted, the "surprise" must be a guest. That wasn't exactly what I was expecting. New shoes, maybe some AirPods, but not someone showing up out of the blue. After what I'd been through today, I wasn't sure I could even handle that kind of surprise. Could this day get any worse? I seriously hope not.

Chapter 13

Tell Me More Lies

The start of my weekend hadn't been going so well. I thought it would get better once I got home. I was wrong. It had gotten seriously, seriously worse.

"What the hell is this, Mom?" I yelled, walking into the house to find Travis, my mom's ex-con, ex-boyfriend laughing it up with her in the kitchen. He was sipping a glass of lemonade while she pawed over him like an excited puppy whose owner just walked in after being gone all day. I wanted to barf.

"Hi, honey," she answered, oblivious to the anger I was projecting. "Remember I told you about a surprise? Well.., surprise!"

She had a smile on her face bigger than I'd seen from her in years, but none of that mattered as I stared down Travis, shooting daggers at him.

"Mom, what is he doing here? How did he find us?"

"Oh, Emma, stop being so dramatic," she replied, brushing my comments off by flopping her hand forward like I was being silly. "We'd been talking with each other for a while now, so I asked him to come."

"Oh my God! That's who you were on the phone with the other day, wasn't it?" I questioned angrily. "Why would you do that, Mom? He tried to kill you."

"Now, wait a minute," Travis spoke up, placing his glass on the center island, "that was all just a misunderstanding. Your mom and I – we worked it out."

"You 'worked it out'? That's it? Mom, he threatened you and chased you around the house with a knife. He wrapped a towel around your neck and tried strangling you to death."

"Honey, that was just the alcohol," she responded, making excuses for his sorry ass. "He's been sober now for over two years."

"That's right," Travis announced, placing his arm around my mom's shoulder and pulling her to his side, "I don't touch the stuff."

"You see, honey?" my mom added.

I looked at her; I looked at him; I looked at her again. I felt my hands ball up in fists.

"Unbelievable, Mom! I can't be around this. I'm going to my room."

I huffed and stormed past them, probably scorching their skin with the heat I was giving off.

"Emma, wait," my mom pleaded.

I heard Travis speak to her in a hushed tone, "Let her go; she'll warm up to me."

Warm up to him, my ass, I thought. It'd be a cold day in Hell before that happened. How could she do that – brush aside all the crap he put her.., put *us* through? I mean, who does that? Was she *that* desperate? Who contacted who first? Grrr!

I charged upstairs, stomping each tread as I did. My words didn't get my point across; maybe my feet would. I couldn't believe how this day was turning out. Friday was supposed to be a day you looked forward to. Instead, I found out my best friend was keeping a secret from me, the police questioned me like I was a suspect, and my mom made the worst decision of her life by letting that asshole into our house. Was I the only sane person? If I packed a bag and threatened to run away, would that make her come to her senses? Wait; scratch that. If she had any sense in that head of hers, she wouldn't have been talking with Travis to begin with.

I was so angry; I needed to occupy my brain with other things. I grabbed my laptop, stretched out on my bed, and surfed the internet. First up was Patti Lynn. Let's see what juicy stuff the World Wide Web had on "the one and only."

I was at it for over half an hour before I found something. I searched through dozens of pages of Patti Lynns across the globe but only found one little tidbit on our fanfic enthusiast, and even that was nothing unusual. It seemed she won a writing contest when she was fifteen and her short story was printed in the local paper. That was it; nothing else. If I wanted to learn more, I'd have to pry it out of her.

After hitting that dead end, I searched for articles from Cameron County, PA. I liked to keep tabs on things that were going on back home. Now and again, something big would hit the news that would make me feel my search efforts were worthwhile. Depending on the story, it would also put my mind at ease.

The web searching did the trick; I forgot all about the uncomfortable situation taking place downstairs. Well, I forgot, that is, until my mom yelled up to me.

"Emma, dinner's ready. Come down and join us."

'*Us?*' I thought. Ugh. There was no '*us*.' At least, not an '*us*' that included that psychopath, Travis.

"I'm not hungry," I yelled back through my closed door. That was a lie; I was starving. I think my stomach was already eating itself.

"Honey, you need to eat something," she insisted.

"No, I don't," I replied bluntly. "Not while *he's* here."

I could almost picture her shaking her head in frustration, letting out a deep sigh. She didn't respond. It was just as well; she'd be wasting her breath.

I stayed in my room the rest of the night, hoping she'd get the hint and toss Travis out on his ear. After a couple of hours, when that didn't happen, I began regretting my decision to skip dinner but was too stubborn to leave the confines of my room. I didn't want to see either of them. Imagine if I went downstairs and caught them making out on the couch. Gross! I wasn't willing to take that chance. All I could do was stop thinking about it, curl up, and go to bed. If she found my body in the morning emaciated from starvation, maybe she'd learn her lesson. On the other hand, if she didn't, well..., at least I would have lost some weight, so it wouldn't have *all* been for nothing.

The cracking sound outside my window woke me up. The morning's shining light, rudely causing my eyes to squint in pain, ensured I'd stay that way. A second loud cracking sound echoed in from outside. I sat up and leaned forward to look out the window through hazy eyes. Travis was in the backyard, holding some long, half-round wooden dowel that looked like a stair railing. He leveraged it on the ground at an angle and stomped on a section of it, breaking it into a shorter length. There were two other pieces like it on the ground by his feet, the very reason for my sleeplessness. I caught myself rolling my eyes. Not because he was in the back-yard making all kinds of noise, but because I guess that meant he stayed the night. That was as far as my thoughts wanted to take it. I wouldn't let my-self think he and my mom did anything nasty while I slept. Crap, I just did. That didn't count. Aaauugh! My mind screamed to get the horrible thought out of my head.

My phone on my nightstand vibrated; a text came through. It was probably from my mom. She had to know how upset I was last night. I certainly didn't disguise my feelings. This was her attempt to try to smooth things over by sending an apolo-gy, followed by some little red hearts or an emoji blowing a kiss. Believe me, Mom, it'd take more than that to make it up to me. You owed me big. And you could start paying up by kicking *him* out.

I swung my legs off the side of the bed and sat for a moment rubbing my eyes, determined to clear all the goo from the inside corners. I thought about how I shouldn't be awake at this ungodly hour. Not that I knew what hour it was, but I knew it was a Saturday, and I was supposed to be able to sleep in on Saturdays. Damn you, Travis, and your stupid wood breaking. You shouldn't even be here.

I shook it off and reached for my phone, cu-rious how my mom planned to try to make things up to me. "Try," being the operative word. It was going to take a lot. But, when I read the text, my heart quickened. A chill ran down my spine. It wasn't from my mom.

How can you live with yourself after what you did?

It was from the same unknown number as the previous text I'd received. It was all just a joke, right? It had to be. My thumbs frantically tapped the virtual keyboard.

Who is this? This isn't funny.

I kept my eyes glued to the screen, waiting for a response. It came.

Neither is what you did.

I felt my breathing become shallow. I couldn't believe what someone was texting me. Just then, I heard the back door close, startling me, and I slammed my phone, screen side down, onto my mattress as if someone had unexpectedly barged into my room and caught me doing something I shouldn't have been doing. Clearly, the strange texts had me rattled.

I stood up and grabbed a pair of lightly used sweatpants from the top of my laundry basket.

Don't judge me; it's Saturday.

I quickly threw the sweats on and stepped out into the hallway to call down to my mom. Though I might not have been too happy with her recent life choices, hearing her voice would still calm my nerves.

"Mom?"

"No, it's me, Travis," his voice rang out, eating away at my soul. "Your mom ran to the grocery store to pick up a few things."

I didn't reply. I just slid back into the comfort of my room. *What the hell, Mom?* I thought. *In whose right mind was it okay to leave me alone with a guy who tried to kill you?* That woman and I needed to have a comprehensive chat about Parenting 101.

I walked to my dresser opposite the bed to grab a clean shirt (day-old sweatpants acceptable, dirty shirt, no way). As I passed by the front window, I noticed my mom's car parked in the driveway. When Travis said she ran to the store, I doubt he meant it in the literal sense. My mom didn't know how to *spell* exercise, let alone partake in the nasty activity. Either she had just pulled in while I was in the hall - which was unlikely since I would have heard her come in by now - or Travis lied to me. There was a third option, of course, which involved Travis being a moron and not realizing my mom was in the next room, but that didn't make sense because she would have said something when she heard me call out. It wouldn't stop me, though, from thinking Travis was a moron.

I threw on the long-sleeved shirt I'd swiped from my top drawer and headed downstairs to abate my curiosity. I walked into the living room to find Travis standing in the far corner, staring at framed pictures on the decorative display unit my mom often bragged about building (if following IKEA instructions could be considered as such). He must have heard me coming down the stairs, though he didn't turn to acknowledge me.

"It looks like you and your mom have had some good times the last couple of years," he said, picking up one of the pictures to get a closer look. "I like this one," he continued, flashing it over his shoulder.

It was a picture of me and my mom from last summer when we vacationed in Virginia Beach. We were strutting along the shore, showing off our fancy matching bikinis. My mom had asked a kindly woman walking her dog if she wouldn't mind taking our picture.

"You've really grown since I last saw you."

My skin crawled at the thought of what Travis might have meant by *"you've really grown."* I didn't want to think about it, instead wishing I had stayed in my room. I quickly changed the subject.

"I thought you said my mom went to the store."

"She did," he replied, placing the picture back in its spot. "She left about fifteen minutes ago."

"Her car's in the driveway," I stated, pointing to the closed window curtains.

"It is?" he said, looking confused.

He made his way to the window and pulled a flap of the curtain aside to see for himself.

"That's weird; I swore she left. She's probably just outside, dilly-dallying. I'll go and check."

He walked out the front door and wandered around the side of the house just out of view. I closed the door, and just as I did, I heard a thumping sound behind me. It sounded like it came from the back hallway.

"Mom?" I hollered.

There was no answer, but I knew I heard something. So, of course, as every slasher movie murder victim thinks to themselves before meeting their inevitable demise, I had to investigate.

As I walked down the hall to the rear of the house, where the door to the basement was, I heard another sound – like something scraping on the floor.

"Mom?" I yelled again, louder this time. "Are you in the basement?"

I opened the door and immediately heard incomprehensible mumbling. I cautiously took a few steps down the stairway until I saw a sliver of my mom's legs duct-taped together and writhing from side to side.

"Mom!" I screamed, bounding down the stairs in an adrenaline-fueled frenzy, my body ignoring the tingling sensation running down my arms and legs. "Oh my God, Mom!"

Chapter 14

The Fear Inside

She was lying on her side on the concrete floor, her arms bound behind her with more duct tape, and another piece covering her mouth and wrapped around her head to hold it in place. Her eyes widened in panicked appreciation when she saw me, and she began to struggle more furiously, letting out muffled screams.

"I got you, Mom; I got you," I cried, trying to calm her down so I could free her. She was twisting and turning so much, making it difficult to get ahold of the tape. "Mom, stop moving."

I grabbed for her wrists first, tugging at the tape, her hands pale from the lack of circulation. There was so much duct tape wrapped around her wrists, and my hands were shaking so wildly that I couldn't tear it free. The tears forming in my eyes didn't help the situation. I quickly scanned the room, looking for something to use to cut the restraints, but I couldn't see anything from my squatted position. I yanked on the tape again, more aggressively, panic gripping my insides. My mom's body flopped, but the tape didn't budge.

"Hold on, Mom!" I shouted, pushing myself up. "I'll find something." My legs were wobbly with fear. Adrenaline was all that carried my weight. I didn't know what to do; I couldn't think straight.

My mind first went to the kitchen to grab a knife, but it was so far away, and I couldn't risk running into Travis. He did this, the son of a bitch. Plus, the thought of leaving my mom alone after who knew how long she'd already been down here.., I couldn't do that.

I frantically scoured the dusty shelves and makeshift workbench until I found an old metal toolbox in the bench cabinet. The box was empty except for a bent pair of pliers and an old box cutter with a rusty blade. It would have to do the trick. I grabbed it and ran back to my mom's side, assuring her I'd cut her free.

"It's okay, Mom; I'm here," was what managed to escape my trembling lips. "I'm going to get you free. Try not to move; I don't want to cut you."

As I cut, I couldn't stop thinking about how awful it'd be if I accidentally sliced her wrist. With my hands quivering as violently as they were while I struggled to hack through the layers of tape, the possibility was frighteningly present. It didn't help that my mom was as scared as I was and kept sporadically wriggling her body, making my task more difficult.

"Mom, stop!" I barked in frustration. "I'm almost through."

She screamed, the awful sound muffled behind a barrier of silver tape. Tears leaked sideways from her eyes and dripped to the concrete below. I hated everything about it. Seeing her like that only made me cry harder.

A few seconds later, the tape around her wrists snapped loose, freeing her hands. She pushed herself upright with her elbow and began wrestling with the tape around her head while I slid down to free her bound ankles. I noticed her hands weren't working properly due to the lack of blood flow, and she kept stopping to shake them, trying to get some feeling back.

"I've almost got it, Mom," I reassured her. "Then, I can help you."

Moments later, her legs were free - as was her ability to speak. I grabbed her arm to help her up as she uttered senselessly.

"I should have listened. I should have listened. You were right, Emma. I should have listened. You were right. I never should have believed him. I let him back in. I let..,"

"It's okay, Mom," I said abruptly, shuffling her to the staircase as quickly as I could. "We've got to get out of here before he comes..,"

My words stopped short, stuck in my throat. It was too late. Standing in the open doorway at the top of the stairs, Travis peered down at us with hatred in his eyes. He was holding one of the pieces of stair railing he'd broken and clenching his teeth.

"No, you're gonna stay down there, sweetheart." he threatened, pointing the stick at us. "Your momma did this to me. She had me locked up like I was a goddamn criminal."

"You *are* a criminal," I yelled defiantly.

"Aren't we all?" he snickered. "Well, now you're gonna see what that shit does to a person," he seethed. "Welcome to *my* brand of prison. Get used to it, ladies; you're going to be down there awhile."

He slammed the door, and I heard him jostling with something. I let go of my mom's arm and dashed up the stairs. The jostling sound stopped. I tried the knob. It freely turned, but when I tried opening the door, it didn't budge, no matter how much I pushed and slammed against it. He must have padlocked the latch on the outside of the door.

"Let us out of here, Travis!" I screamed, pounding on the door.

"Enjoy your stay," he replied, walking away.

"Asshole!" I bellowed.

I charged back downstairs and grabbed my mom's arm.

"The bulkhead," I announced. "It locks from the inside."

"Emma, I'm so sorry, baby," my mom said hysterically. "You were right; you were always right. I should have listened to you. He shouldn't be here. My beautiful baby girl. I'm so sorry."

My mom kept sobbing while "*sorry*" poured out of her mouth over and over through panic-stricken breaths.

"Mom! Not now!" I snapped, rushing to the far side of the basement.

She immediately clammed up, her body language showing I'd caught her off guard with my stern command. I felt bad about it, but I also didn't. I needed her to shut up so I could think.

I hustled up the cement stairs to the bulkhead doors, unlatched them, and gave a shove. I expected them to swing open, freeing us, but instead, they lifted only slightly before slamming back down. I pushed on the doors again, just enough to see a crack of daylight. It was also enough to see what was preventing them from opening. The other two pieces of railing were wedged through the exterior handles, keeping the doors at bay.

"Son of a..," I said, beyond aggravated.

Feeling anxious and panicky, I shot back down the stairs and past my mom, heading for the other staircase again. My mom stood quietly, watching me race around. I ran up to the basement door and began kicking it and slamming my fist against it in a mad frenzy.

"Travis!" I screamed. "Open the door, Travis!" My screams got louder and louder. "Let us out of here, you piece of shit!" I slammed my shoulder into the door. "Travis! Open the door!"

Then, without warning, it was like I had nothing left in me. I felt drained - exhausted. The adrenaline had worn off. I slid my back down the door and sat on the top step, trying to catch my breath. I couldn't believe this was happening; this couldn't be real. And yet, staring down at the cold, concrete floor, feeling every beat of my heart as it crashed into my rib cage, I knew that it was. I couldn't hold back the tears, and I gasped for breaths that weren't there.

There had to be something we could do. Instinctively, I tapped my sweatpants' pockets, hoping I'd tucked my phone into one of them, even though I vividly remembered it lying on my bed. No luck; no phone. Shit! Shit! And that is why, the next time my mom complains that kids these days are too attached to their phones, I get to throw it back in her face.

Crap! My mom. I had to check on her. I had no idea how long she'd been down here. What did Travis do to her?

I pushed myself upright, my left butt cheek in the beginning stages of falling asleep, sending tingles down the back of my leg. I hobbled my way down the stairs to see my mom bent over against the built-in workbench, one hand leveraged on her knee to keep herself from falling forward, the other partially covering her face as she tried desperately to hide her flowing tears.

"Mom?" I said in a quiet voice. "Are you all right? Did he hurt you?"

She shook her head while wiping the tears from her cheeks. "I can't believe I let this happen."

"You didn't do this, Mom." She totally did. "How could you have known?" She should have known. "We're going to get out of this." How the hell were we going to get out of this?

I looked up at the undersized windows overhead, their minuscule size teasing us. I wasn't an expert, and I never had any reason to pay much attention before, but they seemed smaller than the average basement windows. I might have been able to squeeze out of them if I were still eight years old, but that ship had long sailed. Breaking one of them and screaming for help wouldn't do any good. Even if our closest neighbors hadn't already left on their two-week vacation, their house was too far away for anyone to hear our screams. Besides that, it would only alert that maniac Travis, and there's no telling what he would do to us in his current frame of mind.

"He can't keep us down here," I said, trying to reassure myself as much as my mom. "He's just being a dick. He'll let us out in an hour or two. You'll see. It's just a joke. That's it. He's playing mind games with us. Just a sick, pathetic, twisted joke by a sick, pathetic, twisted asshole."

"I'm so sorry, baby," my mom said as she ran her fingers through my hair, valiantly fighting away the tears. "I should have never invited him back into our lives."

That's right; she shouldn't have.

"It's all right, Mom," I responded, grabbing her hand in mine and squeezing. "Everything's going to be all right."

Everything was definitely *not* going to be all right.

"We just need to keep calm."

How the hell does that work?

"He's going to let us out."

He wasn't going to let us out.

Chapter 15

'Til Death Do Us Part

The hours ticked by. How many? I couldn't say. The sun's calming light faded beyond the distant treeline some time ago. If I had to guess, I'd say it'd been about thirteen hours. If you asked my stomach, it'd say a week. I'd just about lost my voice from the screaming. I wasn't yelling for help; that'd be pointless. Instead, I was sticking it to Travis, letting him know all the ways he was a complete asshole for locking us down here.

My mom and I spent a few hours huddled together, trying to keep our bodies from shaking after the emotional rollercoaster we'd already endured and were still enduring. My palms were beet red from smacking them against the door for ten minutes straight. Then, I used my fists until I broke the skin, and they began bleeding and throbbing.

My mom had given up. I wanted to hate her for it, but she'd already been down here for hours before I found her squirming on the floor, barely able to move. She struggled to free herself that entire time. That had to have taken its toll. She was weak, tired, and emotionally drained, thinking she had ruined our lives, and because of it, we'd soon be dead. That wasn't going to happen, though I *was* feeling weak myself. I hadn't eaten anything since lunchtime yesterday. I just *had* to be stubborn and skip dinner last night. Now, I was paying the price. Not that it would have done me any good; I'd still be in this mess, but my stomach wouldn't be growling the national anthem and making other funny noises if I'd only swallowed my pride and eaten a little something.

More than anything else, though, we were dehydrated. My mom's lips were chapped, and my tongue kept sticking to the inside of my mouth. When I tried to lick my lips, it stuck there too. I had no idea how long Travis thought he could keep us down here before somebody came looking, but we needed food and water. Imagine how embarrassing it would be if our would-be rescuers arrived to find only a pile of bones. Hell, even prisoners received three meals a day.

I no sooner finished that thought than Travis yelled from outside the doorway.

"If you want to eat, you'd better stay far away from the door. I want to hear your voices so I know where you are. I mean it. If you so much as step onto the bottom stair, I'll lock it up again, and you'll get nothing. Now start chirping, ladies."

I couldn't believe this. I wanted to charge the door so bad, but I wanted food and drink more. If we went without until morning, we'd barely have enough strength to stand. Logic prevailed.

Loudly, I prompted my mom. "Come on, Mom," I bellowed, "let's tell Travis what a twisted Mother F'er he is." My mom didn't like me swearing in front of her, so Mother F'er was what I landed on.

"He's a dirty piece of shit," she joined in.

"Scumsucking dirtbag," I added.

Back and forth, we yelled our frustration.

"Asshole loser."

"Prick."

"Cocksucker."

"Scumbag."

"Limp dick."

On and on it went until we heard the door slam shut and the jiggling of the padlock hasp.

"You bitches are real funny," Travis yelled through the door. "Keep it up, and you'll *never* get out of there. Enjoy."

Like excited kids on Christmas, we hurried to the stairwell to see what kind of presents Santa had left us. As soon as I saw it, my heart sank.

On the top stair was a single bowl and a glass of water. It wasn't exactly the five-course meal I was imagining. I looked at my mom with disappointment radiating from my facial expression.

"I'll get it."

She forced a smile and rubbed her hand down my back. I walked up the stairs to retrieve the glass and gourmet mystery meal. It was worse than I imagined – macaroni and cheese. The son of a bitch did that on purpose. He must've remembered how much I couldn't stand the stuff. As if that weren't bad enough..,

"You forgot a spoon!" I yelled.

"You have hands," Travis' distant voice returned.

I looked at my mom and shook my head in anger. She waved me down, maintaining her fake composure to keep from breaking down again, knowing damn well she was the one who got us into this predicament. It was all *her* fault. She was the one who fell for his stupid apologies and his made-up stories about how he'd changed. I needed to calm down. Hating on my mom wasn't helping.

We sat on the bottom step, our shoulders together, staring at the dishes I held.

"You go ahead and take a sip," she said to me, nudging my hand that was holding the glass of water.

"No, Mom. You need it more than I do." I handed her the glass, she sipped, then handed it back to me. I took a sip, then placed it on the concrete floor between our feet. I presented her with the bowl of processed, unpronounceable ingredients. She tilted her head and shrugged, then dug two fingers into the orange slop and scooped some slimy noodles into her palm.

"No different than when you were a baby," she said before slapping her palm to her mouth to inhale the disgusting macaroni.

"Oh, it's different," I gagged, digging my own fingers in to gather some of the mush.

We took turns scooping from the bowl until there was nothing left – especially our dignity. I wiped my sticky fingers, first on the bottom stair beside me, then on my sweatpants to remove the remainder of the cheese stains from my nails. My mom licked hers clean. We savored the water, only taking a small sip every ten minutes or so until it, too, was gone.

I found some dusty old cardboard boxes that had been flattened and propped against the wall in the corner. I dragged them out to the middle of the floor, brushed them off, and arranged them into a large square. I figured if we were stuck down here, we might as well get comfortable.

I sat on the large-screen TV box, my mom on the vacuum cleaner box, and we squeezed close, leaning our heads sideways against each other.

"It's all my fault," my mom whispered.

"Don't, Mom," I comforted her. "You can't blame yourself for the actions of that lunatic asshole."

"But if I hadn't..,"

"I don't want to talk about it," I interrupted. "I'm too tired." That wasn't entirely true. I was more afraid I'd say something I'd later regret. It was better to keep quiet.

We sat in silence for the rest of the night.

⧗ ⧗ ⧗

I awoke to the sound of footsteps coming down the stairs. I sprang to a seated position and shook my mom, who was still sound asleep (at least *one* of us was able to get comfortable). She opened her eyes, saw me sitting upright with a terrified look on my face, and pushed herself up onto her elbow.

"What is it, Emma?"

I didn't have to respond as Travis' foot kicked the empty bowl off the bottom step onto the concrete, jolting my mom to her knees. I grabbed her sleeve and stood up, then helped her to her feet.

"Did you two have a nice stay at Chez Travis?" he questioned snidely.

"Let us go, Travis," my mom said through clenched teeth, grabbing my arm and pulling me behind her. "You can't keep us here."

He flashed an uncaring smirk, "And I don't intend to. What, do you think I'm some heartless, wild animal or something?"

"Then why have you done this?" my mom questioned.

"Why do you think?" he replied. "After everything we'd been through, you called the police on me and had me arrested. I went into state lockup because of you. I wanted you to feel what I felt."

"You tried to kill me, you son of a bitch!" my mom yelled. "I loved you."

"Well, I didn't love *you*," he screamed back. "You were just one more piece of ass in a long line of women. Just like the other night.., just another piece of ass for me to enjoy after doing my time."

In a rage, and to my surprise, my mom stepped forward and slapped Travis across the face.

"You goddamn piece of shit!" she yelled, saliva spraying from her mouth. "Get out of my house!"

That probably wasn't the smartest thing to do in the long list of unsmart things my mom had done in the past two days. Travis looked at her with fire in his eyes. We both knew what was coming but were too slow to react. He cocked his arm and punched my mom in the face, knocking her to the ground.

"Mom!" I cried, springing to check on her.

Travis grabbed my shoulder and shoved me aside as he stood over my mom threateningly, pointing his finger.

"You stupid bitch!" he seethed. "I told you I had no intention of keeping you down here. I got what I came for; I was letting you go. But now, I think I'll leave you with a parting gift - something to remember me by." He stepped over her legs and peered down at her. "And when I leave, you'd better not even think about calling the police. They won't find me, but I know where you live now. I can come back any time I want to finish what I started."

Panicking, I whipped my head around, looking for something.., anything to grab. I spotted the box cutter on the floor just behind our cardboard beds and scooped it up. Holding it in both trembling hands, I extended my arms toward Travis' back.

"Stay away from my mom, Travis!"

He turned his head slightly over his shoulder to see me threatening him with the less-than-threatening weapon, then spun around to focus on me.

"What in the hell do you think you're doing?" he questioned, stepping toward me.

"I mean it, Travis. Stay away from her, or I'll cut you."

"You ain't gonna do shit, little girl," he said, taking another step forward. "You're more likely to cut yourself."

He swatted my hands, causing me to lose my grip on the makeshift weapon, sending it across the room. With my hands empty, he lunged forward, grabbed me around my throat with one hand, and shoved me backward into the hard concrete wall, maintaining his grasp on my neck. I gasped for air but could barely inhale from his tight grip.

"You would threaten me like that, you little whore?" he barked, his foul breath washing over my face. "I always thought you were the nice one."

He glanced down between us and smiled.

"I guess you'll have to make it up to me," he said, sliding his available hand down the front of my shirt and licking his lips. "Maybe I'll get myself an in-person look at that bikini body of yours?"

I squirmed at his touch, trying to release his hand from around my neck, but it was no use. I felt myself quickly fading from lack of oxygen. He glared at me with a nasty grin just before his head jolted forward and his grip loosened. He made a funny gurgling sound. I watched his eyes roll up into his eyelids as his body crumpled to the floor. Standing behind him with a look of fear in her eyes, my mom stood unsteady, the metal toolbox in her hand, its lower corner painted with Travis' blood. I reached for my neck, sucking in as much air as I could, and looked down at Travis' unmoving body, blood trickling from the opening in the back of his head.

"Mom?"

It was at that moment I witnessed something I had never seen before. My mom's expression became crazed, animalistic.

"Don't you *ever* touch my daughter!" she screamed, raising the toolbox over her head. Before I could stop her (or maybe I didn't want to), she swung the toolbox down repeatedly, smashing it against his head, over and over, until it wasn't a head anymore.

"Mom!" I screamed. "Stop it! Stop it! Mom!"

And then she did. I think it was my voice that stopped her more than my words. But it was too late. The unthinkable had already taken place. My mom's chest heaved in and out as she tried to catch her breath. She dropped the blood-spattered toolbox to the floor, the crashing sound having no impact on either of us. How could it? We'd already been through hell. Or maybe we were still there. We were both standing over Travis' dead body.

Chapter 16

The Best Laid Plans

"**W**hat have I done?" my mom cried, covering her mouth with her blood-stained hands. "What have I done?"

"Calm down, Mom!" I said assertively, leading her away from the body, though we both continued to stare.

"I killed him," she mumbled. "I just reacted."

"Mom, it's going to be okay. Let me think for a minute."

"We have to call the police," she continued hysterically. "He's dead. I killed him. He's dead."

"Mom!" I shouted. "Stop it; you're freaking me out. We can't call the police."

"What do you mean we can't call the police? We have to. He's dead. Travis is dead."

"We can't, Mom," I said more aggressively. "Look at what you did to him."

She looked at me with sorrowful eyes, "But it was self-defense; he was going to kill us."

I didn't think that was true. Beat my mom – maybe. Get his jollies off fondling me – probably. But I don't think he was here to kill us.

"Mom, look at him," I said. "That wasn't self-defense. Maybe the first hit was. After that, we could have gotten away. What you did would be considered excessive and unnecessary." I learned that in my Law and Justice class in my junior year. "There's nothing left of his head, Mom! We can't call the police. They'll put you away for man-slaughter, or, since you invited him here, they could claim it was premeditated. Then they've got you on first-degree murder charges."

"Murder?" she questioned, her voice quivering.

"Yes, murder," I repeated. "You'll go to jail probably for the rest of your life."

"But who would take care of you?" she questioned, her eyes filling with tears.

"You're not listening to me, Mom. We're not calling the police. Travis just got out of jail recently. There's no way he told anybody he was coming here. He probably wasn't supposed to leave the state. And there's nobody around here that knows him."

"What are you saying?" she questioned.

"I'm saying go upstairs and wash yourself up, put on some tea, and let me think of something."

"But baby," she started, shaking her head and crying harder, "you can't stay down..,"

"Mom!" I stopped her from continuing. I gently grabbed the sides of her face in my hands and stared into her leaking eyes. "I've got this." I nodded to let her know of my confidence before stating it a second time. "I've got this, Mom. Now, go." I dropped my hands from her cheeks and gestured my head toward the stairwell. She stared at me for a few seconds longer, trembling, before slowly turning and walking away, her head dipped to her chest. Deep down, she knew I was right. I'm glad one of us did. I had no idea what we were going to do. I wasn't even sure how I was keeping so calm. I wanted to scream out - get all the turmoil and fear out of me, but that would only panic my mom more.

I listened for the door to open and her shadow to disappear from the stairwell before I was able to take a breath. It was all I could do to keep from breaking down, but I had to be the strong one; my mom was an emotional wreck.

I turned to face the gruesome sight my mom left in her furious wake, then immediately closed my eyes.

"Shit! Shit!" I whispered to myself. "Come on, Emma; pull yourself together. You can do this."

I opened my eyes, looked at Travis' practically headless corpse, then began to scan around the room. I needed to get rid of the body. And not *just* the body, but the car, too. I could do both at the same time. That was going to require my mom's help. She wasn't going to like it. Too bad; this was her fault.

Okay, this would require a lot of planning. Luckily, I'd seen enough of these types of movies to piece together what had to get done. My mind was racing a mile a minute. We'd have to dump the body somewhere and stash the car somewhere else. They couldn't be connected. It wasn't like we could drive around with a dead body during the day, so we'd have to do it later tonight after dark. That would give me plenty of time to map things out.

We'd have to erase any trace of Travis ever being here. I looked down at his caved-in head and the pool of blood surrounding it and felt my heart rate increase. It wasn't going to be easy. I'd need some supplies from the store to clean that mess up. For now, I needed to get what was left of his head off the cement. The longer it stayed there, the harder it would be to clean up.

I pulled my sleeves over my hands, bent over, and grabbed Travis' arm. I tugged lightly at first, not knowing what to expect. As it turned out, what they say about dead weight is true; it's heavy. I put a little muscle into it on my second attempt and dragged his body sideways until his head was on the flattened vacuum cleaner cardboard. I moved the television cardboard aside to keep it from getting any blood on it; I'd need it later. That was about all I could do for now, at least, until we picked up those needed supplies. That was when the real work would begin. I wasn't looking forward to it. As it was, I was barely maintaining my composure. What would I be like when it came to..?

I didn't want to think about it.

I ran upstairs to check on my mom and to get ready for a trip to the store. She was sitting at the kitchen table, her head propped up between her fists, staring down at her mug of tea. Her hands were clean of the blood, and she'd changed her clothes. I was happy to see she'd listened to me for a change.

"Are you all right, Mom?" Dumb question. I already knew the answer.

She didn't look up, only nodded her head. I knew it was killing her inside. I put my hand on her shoulder to let her know I was there for her.

"It's going to be fine," I said. "We're going to straighten this all out. It'll be like nothing ever happened." Only, it *did* happen, and nothing would ever be 'fine' again.

She nodded again, but I wasn't sure she was even listening to a word I said.

"I'm going to get changed," I continued. "Then we need to go to the store."

She was unresponsive. I let my hand slip from her shoulder as I walked away, glancing back to see if she'd budged. She didn't. I hustled up to my room to get some clean clothes on. I'd shower later; there was too much to do, and nighttime would arrive faster than expected.

I whipped my sweatpants off and had just finished slipping on a pair of jeans when I heard a car door shut outside my window. I glanced out and saw Detective Harrison making his way up the driveway.

"Oh, shit! What is he doing here?" I mumbled to myself, my heart racing. My legs began trembling uncontrollably. Now what?

Chapter 17

All Lies

I quickly grabbed a cardigan, threw it over my shirt, hoping it didn't look too weird, then swiped my phone from the bed where I'd left it the day before. I needed to get downstairs to intercept my mom before she opened the door. In her current frame of mind, there was no telling what she would say or how she'd react when she learned there was a detective at our door. I didn't have a chance to tell her about the excitement from Friday since my mind was a little too preoccupied with the whole Travis situation. It's amazing how being locked in the basement against your will can make you forget about the trivial things in life. Not that Sabrina's death was trivial by any means, but when stacked against what we were going through, the rest took a back seat. It was funny how brains worked like that in times of stress. Not that I thought to tell her prior, either. I was too angry with her and couldn't look at her.

The doorbell chimed as I got to the top of the stairs. I heard my mom's chair slide out from under the table, and I raced down, hoping to catch her before she opened the door. She was already acting a little unstable. If I was fast enough, I could explain most of it to her before the detective triggered her even more.

I rounded the stair railing to see her already almost at the door. I called out to her in an elevated whisper. You know, the kind you hoped only the intended person could hear.

"Mom, Mom, Mom – wait."

She stopped herself from reaching for the doorknob as I ran to her side to prepare her.

"You should know there's been a..," I froze mid-whisper, my eyes locked onto my mom's chin. "Shit! You have dried blood on your chin."

Her eyes widened. She looked in the mirror by the door, licked her first two fingers, then aggressively rubbed away the last of the incriminating evidence just as the doorbell rang a second time. I shot her a grimace.

"Stay calm, and don't say anything about Travis," I whispered.

She nodded, but again, expressionless as if she hadn't understood my words. I wasn't feeling confident she could keep it together. She opened the door to greet our visitor while I leaned my head against the edge of the door to appear innocent.

"May I help you?" my mom greeted.

I jumped right in, "Detective Harrison? What are you doing here? Did you find out anything more about Sabrina's case?"

"Hello, Emma," he said, flashing his charming smile, already trying to weaken my resolve. "And you must be Emma's mother," he continued, turning his voodoo magic on my mom. "I'm sorry to bother you. As your daughter mentioned, I'm Detective Harrison." He pointed to the badge clipped to his belt. My eyes couldn't help drifting to the front of his pants, where, to the left of his zipper, I could almost make out the outline of his.., *Stop it, Emma*, my mind screamed. "Your daughter and I spoke in the principal's office on Friday."

"You did?" my mom questioned. "And why would a detective need to speak with my daughter?"

"Oh, your daughter didn't tell you?"

My mom gave me a side-eyed glare. "No, she didn't. But we've been pretty busy this weekend. I'm sure it just slipped her mind."

"Graduation is coming up in a few weeks," I jumped in. "We're trying to get things ready for it."

"I understand," he nodded. "To answer your question, Mrs. Murphy.., I'm sorry, is it Mrs. or Ms.?"

"It's Erin," she replied.

Oh my God, Mom, I thought. *Are you falling for his charisma and undeniable good looks?*

"Erin. Got it." He smiled again. "We've been investigating a student's death..,"

"A student's death?" my mom gasped. "Oh my God. How awful."

At least, now my mom had a good reason for seeming a little out of it. That eased my mind slightly.

"Yes," Detective Harrison responded. "Very unfortunate. That's why we thought it important to speak with some of the student's friends and their families."

"May I ask how the student died? Should I be worried for my daughter's safety?"

"I'm afraid I can't discuss the details of the case, but we believe it was an isolated incident. You and Emma have nothing to worry about."

"Thank goodness," my mother responded, placing her hand on her chest.

I couldn't believe she was keeping it together. Good for her. Great for us. Then the detective asked the question I was dreading.

"If you wouldn't mind, may I come in for a moment? I have a few more questions I'd like to ask Emma if it's not too much trouble. I could have asked that you come down to the station, but I didn't want to worry you for no reason. I thought it best if I stopped by in person."

Before my mom could answer, I stated excitedly, "We were actually just on our way out."

"I understand," he said. Then he looked at my mom for *her* approval. "I promise, Erin; It'll only take a minute of your time."

Ugh! He threw her name in there to elicit a positive response. I see the little game you're playing, mister. It won't work; my mom understands what our priority is, and that's getting Travis and his car far away from here.

"Okay," my mom replied, "but only for a few minutes. We have some important errands that absolutely must get done today."

She caved? *What is wrong with you, Mom? Do you not get that there's a dead body in our basement right now? Shit, did I close the basement door?*

"Thank you, Erin," Detective Harrison said as he stepped through the door. "I'll make this as brief as I can."

The detective's eyes scanned around the room.

"This is a beautiful home you have here."

"Thank you," my mom replied. "We moved here a little over six months ago."

"From Pennsylvania?" he questioned.

My mom gave him a curious glare.

He threw his thumb over his shoulder, "I noticed the car out front had Pennsylvania plates. That's a pretty sweet ride. What is it, an '87 Camaro?"

"That's my uncle's car," I blurted. "He's been visiting for the week."

"Oh, is he here?" the detective asked. "I'd love to ask him how it handles."

My mom took the lead on that one. "He's upstairs taking a nap. He's heading back home later today. Long drive."

"Ah, I see," he responded. "I'm sorry, but can I trouble you for a glass of water?"

"Sure," my mom nodded, waving him forward. "Why don't we sit in the kitchen?"

"Thank you," he replied.

He looked at me and drew his hand forward to let me go ahead of him. Oh, sure; good looks, *and* he's a gentleman. Could it get any worse?

Following my mom, I led him into the kitchen and sat in the chair opposite the sink. He sat in the chair to my right and folded his hands on the table. My mom poured him a glass of water from the tap, but when she turned to place it on the table, her hand was shaking wildly. I noticed Detective Harrison's concerned stare and immediately reached forward and took the glass from my mom's hand, placing it down in front of him.

"Mom, did you forget to take your medication this morning?"

"What?" she questioned, glancing at me confusedly. "Oh, right. My medication. If you'll excuse me for a moment."

She stepped away, ducking into the bathroom, leaving me to pick up the pieces. I smiled awkwardly at the detective, shaking my head.

"I'm always reminding her."

He displayed an uncomfortable grin, then took a sip from his glass.

"So, what else did you need to ask me?" I inquired, anxious to get this over with.

"Right to it, huh?" he said, placing the glass back on the table. "Okay, how well do you know your classmates?"

Oh boy, if that wasn't a loaded question. You wouldn't believe the kind of dirt I had on half of the student body.

"Not that well," I replied. "I mean, I haven't been here that long."

"Right," he responded, nodding. "But how well do you know Miss Lynn?"

"Patti?" I questioned. "I know her a little. We don't hang out or anything. She's a.., unique character, that's for sure."

Just then, my mom emerged from the bathroom and sat down across from the detective.

"I'm sorry about that, Detective Harrison," she said with a quaint smile. "I'm feeling better now."

"It's quite all right," he replied.

I turned my attention back to him to get back on track. "Wait, why are you asking me about Patti, anyway? You don't think..? I mean, you said she was with Mrs. Donaldson that night."

"Well, Mrs. Donaldson reached out to us later that night. It turns out she had her days confused."

"Patti Lynn," my mom spoke, directing her words toward me. "Isn't that the girl you said was a little strange and was always spreading gossip around the school?”

“Yeah, but she’s harmless,” I replied. “I think she’s just desperate for friends.” I turned back to Detective Harrison, “Anyway, I don’t think..,”

My thoughts were interrupted by my vibrating back pocket. Without thinking, I pulled my phone out and looked at the text.

```
They will catch you, you know.
```

“Is everything all right?” Detective Harrison questioned, probably noticing how white my face must have become.

“Oh, yeah, fine,” I responded, tucking my phone back into my pocket. “It was just a reminder that we *really* needed to get going if we were going to make it on time.” I glared at my mom with a concerned look on my face. “Mom, we need to go or we’re going to miss it.”

My mom did her part by looking up at the clock on the wall.

“Oh, right,” she said. “I do apologize, detective, but if there’s nothing else, we really must be going.”

“I understand,” he nodded, pushing himself up from his chair. “I won’t keep you any longer.”

“Let me walk you out,” my mom said, stepping around the table.

We escorted him to the door, where he turned before exiting, "Thank you for your time, Erin. Emma. Oh, and I should point out, depending on our findings, we may need Emma to come down to the station at some point to give a formal state-ment." He reached into his pocket, pulled out a card, and handed it to my mom. "If you think of anything else or hear something at school, you can reach me at that number."

"Thank you, Detective," my mom said.

"Yeah, thanks," I followed, rushing him out.

He stepped away and I shut the door, pressing my back to it.

"Don't ask," I said quietly. "We've got our own problems. Let's get ready."

Chapter 18

Shopping Spree

"This isn't the time, Mom!" I stated heatedly as we pulled into the Big W Superstore. It was the second time in five minutes she'd asked about the incident regarding Sabrina's death. I couldn't give her information the first time she asked. Why would she think anything had changed? I get she's frazzled, but we've got more important things that require attention. Namely, there's a freaking dead body in our basement that we need to dispose of.

"Look," I continued, "I get that you're worried because a student got killed, but you heard Detective Harrison; he said it was an isolated incident. I'm not in any danger." *Not from that, anyway*, I thought.

I noticed the back of her hands turn white as she gripped the steering wheel harder.

"I just wish you would have told me," she replied.

I turned my head away to look out the passenger-side window. Disgusted, I spoke under my breath. "Well, I wish you hadn't brought that scumbag back into our lives, but here we are."

"That isn't fair," she responded.

Oops, I guess it wasn't under my breath *enough*. I turned back and gave my mom an angry look.

"Really? The man tried to kill you – and two other women before - or did you forget? He duct-taped you and locked us both in the basement for over twenty-four hours. He punched you in the face and was ready to do more. He choked me and would have done who knows what else. And then, you decided smashing his head in would be a good idea. I'm here wracking my brain trying to think of what we need to clean up the mess *you* created, but you would rather talk about a student who got herself killed. I can't deal with all this."

Things went woefully silent. My mom parked in a space next to the cart return and stared out her window. I could see her eyes were beginning to tear up. My heart sank. My mom wasn't like me. She couldn't handle this kind of stress. On top of everything else, I didn't need her drawing attention to us by breaking down in a crowded parking lot. I had to change the mood.

"The worst part was, I had to eat macaroni and cheese. That's the *real* tragedy here."

I saw a grin appear on my mom's face. She glanced over at me and broke into a chuckle. I returned an awkward smile.

"Now come on," I said, nudging my head sideways, "we've got a lot of work to do."

She sniffed in whatever snot was about to leak from her nose and quickly wiped her eyes with her sleeve.

"Okay, let's go," she returned, nodding.

I told her to act natural as we wandered down the aisles, looking for the items on the list stored in my head. It's not like we could buy a 50-gallon drum and some sulfuric acid, or a pallet of lye, or a carriage full of plastic wrap and a hacksaw. Those are good items for most TV show cleanups, but all very specific things that even the Scooby-Doo gang would find suspicious. We had to be more random than that.

My list seemed more like your average, everyday shopper's impulse buys. We had a bag of kitty litter, a comforter, a bread knife, some golf gloves, a quart of motor oil, two plastic beach pails with a plastic shovel, and a baseball hat. I thought it was clever. Sherlock Holmes would have a difficult time connecting the dots on those items.

When we got to the checkout, I told my mom to pay with cash; we didn't need any credit card transaction history coming back to haunt us. So far, everything was going smoothly, but that was all the easy stuff. It would hit harder once night crept in, when things became more real.

On the ride home, we began brainstorming about secluded areas where we could dump Travis' body (like it was a typical Sunday afternoon, and we were talking about places to vacation). We couldn't just toss him on the side of the road somewhere, though that's about all he deserved. We couldn't throw him in the river; he would wash up somewhere, or some unlucky fisherman would reel the body in, thinking he had himself a big catch. There was no way I was staying out all night, digging a hole deep enough to throw him in. No, we just needed to bring him deep into the woods, somewhere far away from any hiking trails, and scatter some leaves on him. Our thoughts both landed on the woods adjacent to the water treatment plant on the edge of town.

The accessway to the plant was out of the way, about a half mile down a secluded dirt road. The facility itself was fenced in, with security cameras keeping watch. Fortunately, we wouldn't need to get that close. It was perfect.

Shopping list: check.

Location: check.

And, as we pulled into the driveway, with Travis' muscle car staring me in the face, the idea of adding another check to the list made my stomach flop.

It was time for the serious shit.

Chapter 19

It All Goes Away

My mom wasn't getting out of this without getting her hands dirty - figuratively speaking, of course; that's what the golf gloves were for. We had to be cautious. I'd already been questioned about my fingerprints being at a crime scene. That was enough for me. I wanted to make sure everything about *this* disaster disappeared in case the police ever felt they had a reason to come calling. Which they wouldn't.

My mom laid out the comforter on the floor beside Travis, trying her best to avert her eyes from the damage she'd caused to a human skull. But then I opened my big mouth.

"There's so much blood," I said, ensuring her curious glance.

The good news, if there was such a thing, was that the blood had since stopped leaking from Travis' crushed head. The red pool around him had thickened and was now a gooey consistency. Still disgusting. We rolled him onto the blanket, taking care to keep any more blood from dripping onto the concrete. Before wrapping him up, there was something else I needed to do. I told my mom it might be a good time for her to leave the basement, but she insisted on staying. She said whatever it was, she would endure it with me. The thing was, I don't think she was prepared for me to grab the bread knife.

If anyone should come across Travis' body out there in the woods, we couldn't afford authorities being able to ID him. He was forever linked to my mom. We didn't have to worry about his dental records; my mom took care of that when she smashed his face in with the toolbox. But something had to be done about his fingerprints.

I only needed to cut the tips of his fingers off at the first knuckle, so I figured it wouldn't be too difficult. I thought the knife's serrated edge would cut through it like a hacksaw would have. I underestimated how strong bone could be. The skin was easy, but the knife got stuck when it first penetrated the knuckle. I had to pull it out and start again. I put a little more muscle into it the second time. The metal made a screeching sound as the bone rubbed against the side of the blade. It was still better than the cracking sound we heard as the bone snapped in two. I almost threw up. I looked at the severed finger and silently cursed my mom. I still had nine more to go.

Needless to say, it took longer than expected.

After Travis' fingers were removed, I tossed them into the plastic beach pail, and we wrapped what was left of him tightly in the blanket. Mom wanted to use the duct tape to secure the blanket from coming undone, but I told her that wouldn't be necessary. It would be better if we dumped his body without the blanket to let the animals and nature take its course. The tape would only make it harder to get him out.

I then used the blood-stained knife to cut out four slots, two on each side of the flattened TV cardboard box, to use as handholds. We dragged Travis' blanketed body onto the cardboard, ready for transport. If blood seeped through the blanket, the cardboard was an added barrier. We wouldn't want any trace of blood in the back of the vehicle.

It wasn't quite dark enough outside to leave yet, which was fine because there was still more to do inside. I grabbed the pails and shovel and asked my mom to open the kitty litter. She handed the open bag to me, and I poured a hefty amount onto the pool of blood that hadn't dried yet where Travis' head had lain bleeding on the concrete. I let it sit for a couple of minutes, having the litter soak up all it could before I started scooping. The small plastic pail filled quickly. I then opened the quart of oil and poured it all over the bloody stain, followed by more kitty litter to absorb it. The oil stain would easily mask the blood stain. After more time elapsed, I scooped that up into the second pail. Once the cleanup was through, I placed the pails aside to be dealt with later. I glanced up at the basement windows and saw darkness staring back. I looked at my mom and nodded.

"It's time."

No more tears fell from her eyes. She was probably numb to it all after everything we'd done to prepare for this moment. She'd regret it later, but for now, it was what we needed.

"Stay here," I said. "I'll be right back."

I raced upstairs and out the back door to remove the pieces of wood Travis had wedged under the bulkhead handles, then opened both doors. I ran down the concrete steps and stood beside Travis' wrapped body near his head.

"Grab the other side," I said, reaching down to take hold of the slots on my end.

"You sure we can do this?" my mom asked, bending down to grab her side.

"We have to," I answered. "Just take it slow and easy – one step at a time."

I knew the cardboard was durable enough; it was thick and doubled up. I hoped our backs were as sturdy. I raised my eyes to look at my mom, both of us squatting into position.

"Are you ready?"

She nodded.

I took a deep breath and let it out.

"One, two, three!"

We both lifted the dead weight to about our knees. I purposely took the heavier end. As I mentioned before, my mom wasn't exactly the exercise type. I wasn't sure she had the muscle for it. Slowly, carefully, step by agonizing step, we made our way up and out into the backyard, where we lowered Travis to the ground so we could take a break. I closed the bulkhead doors and looked at my mom to see if she was doing okay. I didn't know if it was a late rush of adrenaline or if she'd been secretly lifting weights in her spare time, but she didn't appear as tired as *I* felt. That was fine; I didn't want her having a stroke or something.

"Can you check around the front to make sure it's clear?" I asked, hoping to sit for a moment to catch my breath. It dawned on me that I still hadn't eaten anything for two days except for the few palmfuls of slimy macaroni. That had to be why I was feeling so drained.

"Yeah, good idea," she agreed.

While she took the walk, I sat on the edge of the bulkhead foundation and stared at the rolled-up blanket. There was a body in there. Sure, a no-good, dirtbag, asshole body - but a body, nonetheless. I'd kept my mind busy for so long that I didn't give myself a chance to give it much thought. A man was dead - a man my mom killed. And we were covering it up. What the hell were we doing? I doubted this was what most people considered a mother/daughter bonding moment.

"There's nobody," my mom's voice echoed off the rear of the house, drawing my thoughts back from the brink of insanity.

"Okay," I said, pushing myself up. "Let's go."

We resumed our positions at each end of the robust cardboard and lugged the wrapped body to the rear of Travis' fancy car before it dawned on me.

"Shit!"

"Hey, language," my mother scolded.

"Mom.., dead body. Get over it."

That silenced her.

"Set him down," I said.

"What's the matter?" she asked, lowering her side to the ground.

"The keys," I replied. "We need the keys."

"Oh shit," she let out.

I shot her a nasty glare. "*Language*, Mom."

She gave it right back to me. "I'm the adult here."

"Ummm, hello, I'm eighteen."

She huffed and shook her head. She was at that stage in life where she was still clinging to the thought I was a little girl, but she also knew I wasn't and had to let me go. I imagined it burned her up inside.

"They'd be in his pants pocket," she told me, making little effort to take the lead. I guess that meant it was all on me. Again. *Still.*

I unraveled Travis' rigor-mortised carcass, trying to think of anything else but that. It wasn't working. His stiff body flopped sideways, making a thump sound as it flipped over. I peeled away just enough of the blanket to expose what we needed.

"He was *your* boyfriend," I said, standing back up. "*You* dig the keys out of his pocket. After all, you're the adult here, remember?"

After giving me a sour look, she reluctantly did it. And thank God, too. Gloves or not, I didn't want to risk my fingers touching his junk.

She stood back up, smirked at me, and jingled his keys in her fingers as if to make a point. I rolled my eyes and crouched back down to cover him back up.

"Oh yeah, you're the adult, all right," I stated sarcastically, under my breath. "Now, open the trunk."

She did so, and we heaved the cardboard stretcher carrying Travis' body into the trunk and closed the lid.

I snatched the keys from her. "I'll follow you. Don't drive too fast."

It was an unnecessary reminder. My mom never drove fast. That's why she was taking the lead. We couldn't afford to get pulled over.

She got in her car and began to back out when I excitedly rapped on her window.

"Wait!" I said. "I almost forgot."

I quickly ran into the house and upstairs to my bedroom. I dug an old flannel shirt from the back of my dresser drawer and slung it over my shoulder. On my way back out, I grabbed the baseball hat and threw it on my head. *Now* I was ready.

Seventeen minutes later, we pulled onto the access road and drove for about a quarter of a mile before pulling to the side of the road at the edge of the wooded area. I looked to my right out the passenger-side window into the dark, dense forest. Somewhere out there was to be Travis' final resting place. Somewhere out there was our chance at salvation from this horrible situation we found ourselves in. Somewhere out there was..,

"Hey," my mom's words startled me, her knuckles knocking on the driver-side window. "Are we doing this?"

Earlier in the day, she seemed too distraught to function. Now, she seemed ever too eager to complete this clandestine mission with me. I wished she'd make up her mind.

I opened the door and stepped out. I wasn't sure if the chill I suddenly felt was from the cool air washing over me or the thought of what we were about to do.

"Let's get this over with quickly," I responded. *Before I completely fall apart*, my thoughts added.

I threw on the flannel shirt and popped open the trunk. One of Travis' hands was exposed, and my first thought was, *what a horrible rewrap job I'd done.* Not *gross.* Not, *I can't believe this is happening.* Nope, none of that. What did that say about me?

"Let's leave the cardboard," I said, reaching in to grab hold of the blanket at Travis' shoulders.

My mom took hold of his legs, and we wrestled his stiff body from the trunk. We shuffled our way into the woods, doing our best to avoid dropping the body. The leaves and sticks and uneven ground underfoot weren't making it easy.

After about ten minutes of arduous walking and weaving around obstacles, we arrived at our destination. It wasn't anywhere particular, but it was as good a place as any. It was far enough in the trees that someone would have to work really hard at finding it. Who would do that? Nobody in their right mind would come walking out in these woods. Well, not unless they had a dead body to hide. But then, they wouldn't be in their right mind, would they? Oh, hello; that's us right now.

"Okay, here," I said, dropping my end, unable to carry the dead weight (or my dead arms) any farther. "This will do."

My mom dropped her side, and we pulled at the blanket, letting Travis roll from it onto the ground. We scooped up surrounding leaves and covered him up as well as we could, and then, without saying any final words, we made our way back to the dirt road and our vehicles. I tossed the blanket onto the cardboard in the open trunk and slammed it shut.

"Okay, now you follow me," I said.

That was it. We were in the final stretch. I kept reminding myself that it would all soon be over.

Chapter 20

Shattered Illusions

When the alarm on my phone blared out its annoying wake-up call, I wanted to smash it. Anyone else would have had enough sense to skip school after only three hours of sleep, though I'm not sure the restless tossing and turning I did could be considered sleep. Whatever. I didn't want to draw any unnecessary attention to the Murphy household. I sat up in bed, my eyes still half-closed while images from the previous night flashed in my head.

"Follow you where?" my mom questioned. "Aren't we going back home?"

"Not yet. We have to make one more stop."

"Why? We did it; it's over."

"We have to ditch the car," I reminded her.

I watched her shoulders drop in defeat, having thought the nightmare was over. Not quite yet. But almost.

"Now, follow me. I'll call you along the way to explain."

I hopped in the Camaro and watched my mom over the side mirror as she somberly made her way to her vehicle. I think she was finally coming down off that adrenaline high. It was now reality's turn to smack her in the face.

I slid my butt off the bed and dragged my way to the bathroom. I knew I was asking a lot, but if I had any intention of functioning today, the shower would have to work overtime to wake my sorry, ragged ass. It was a tall task.

I turned the water on full-blast and waited for it to get steamy before stepping under its soothing warmth. The water did wonders, but it couldn't erase the invasive thoughts drilled into my brain.

I parked in the middle row, tucked between two mid-size SUVs. It was an inconspicuous location in the middle of the Big W Superstore parking lot. Not too close, not too far. My mom parked two rows away as I had instructed her to do. I had it all figured out. You always saw in the movies where the bad guys ditched the car on a deserted road or some other out-of-the-way place. The cops always managed to find it, and since it was in a suspicious location, they always investigated and found the criminals. That wasn't going to be us.

The twenty-four-hour superstore always had shoppers in the wee hours of the night. I didn't know where those shoppers came from or why they weren't sleeping. Maybe I didn't want to know. Whatever the case, whatever the time, the parking lot always had vehicles in it. A car didn't look suspicious if it was in plain sight, surrounded by other vehicles at a shopping complex. It was just another late-night customer browsing the aisles.

I tucked my hair under the baseball cap and exited the car, keeping my head down. If there were cameras in the lot, I wasn't about to let them easily recognize me after all my careful planning. I walked into the store and headed straight for the bathrooms. Sadly, there was to be no shopping for this girl.

When I saw it was all clear, I removed the flannel shirt and baseball cap and tossed them into the trash, burying them under a pile of used paper towels. Then, I walked out of the store and calmly strolled a couple of rows down to where my mom's car was still idling. We pulled out of the parking lot, leaving Travis' car and our troubles behind.

I stepped from the shower, wishing I had another ten minutes to spare. I heard my mom stirring downstairs. How could she be so awake? Maybe she never slept. That would be my guess. If her mind was anything like mine, it was torturing her, replaying everything back, hammering against the inside of her skull. She was probably worried sick that we'd forgotten something. *Don't worry, Mom,* I thought. *I took care of it all.*

When we arrived back home, I told my mom to go inside and stay upstairs. I'd handle the cleanup in the basement. She went in the side door; I went around back to go down the bulkhead. It didn't seem as creepy anymore with the dead body gone. Go figure.

I looked at the stain on the floor, and, as I'd hoped, it looked like a harmless, ordinary oil spill. The stain on the vacuum cleaner box, however, looked like a blood stain. That would need rectifying. I grabbed the bread knife off the floor and cut the cardboard into small strips. I felt like an office employee shredding illegal documentation before the authorities came to confiscate it. I then hauled the incriminating cardboard outside and tossed it all into the recycling barrel. Back downstairs again, I grabbed the plastic shovel and kitty-litter-filled beach pails and brought them outside behind our small garden shed. I swiped a spade shovel from its spot within and dug a sizeable hole. After pouring both pails' contents into the hole, I covered it back up. I hung the spade back in place and walked to the back of the house, where the garden hose and outside faucet were located. I washed the pails and shovel and brought them back down the bulkhead into the basement. Everything was just about complete. I stood the pails upside down and jumped on them, smashing them into pieces. I collected the bread knife, the empty bag of kitty litter, the empty quart of oil, and all the shattered plastic and threw it away in the trash upstairs, along with our golf gloves.

Mission accomplished. I could now safely and officially puke my brains out.

I finished getting ready for school and headed downstairs to greet my mom in the kitchen. She was leaning against the counter, rubbing her forehead intensely, her eyes closed, unaware I was even there.

"Mom, what's the matter?" I questioned. "Did you get any sleep?"

She looked up at me, her eyes bloodshot with fear. Why did she look so worried? I did what I said I'd do. I took care of everything. There was nothing to be worried about. We were in the clear.

"The blanket!" she said. "We forgot the blanket."

Shit! The blanket.

Chapter 21

Dead Ahead

I didn't know why I let my mom rattle me like that. I tried to explain to her when she drove me to school that the blanket didn't matter. It was tucked safely away in the Camaro's trunk. As long as the police didn't investigate the car, it wasn't a problem. Obviously, the car couldn't stay there forever; it was only there until we could think of a better idea. I told her if she was that worried about it, we could always go back and grab it from the trunk. I think that eased her mind. Now, if only somebody would ease mine. How could I have been so stupid?

As I walked down the hall on my way to home-room, I saw Liza in her usual stance, kicking at her backpack, trying to force it into the base of her locker. I never got the chance to apologize to her for reacting the way I had when I learned she and Sabrina were seeing each other. Now was as good a time as any.

And it would have been, too, if it weren't for the commotion that suddenly erupted behind me, drawing my attention away.

"Tell us, you little freak!" Jill's voice screamed out.

I turned and witnessed Patti getting shoved back against a locker, the three blonde cheerleaders surrounding her like a pack of hungry hyenas ready to pounce on their prey. I didn't like those odds. I stormed over to defend Patti but wasn't fast enough to prevent Trina from knocking the books out of Patti's hands; papers scattered across the floor in all directions.

"Hey!" I shouted. "Knock it off."

The girls turned to face me at first with a look of shock, thinking a teacher had caught them. Then their expressions turned to relief and finally anger.

"Oh, so you've come to defend your little sick friend?"

"I'm not sick," Patti softly responded.

"Zip it, nerd," Jill barked.

"And she's *definitely* not little," Trina added to her friend's offensive slur.

"Why don't you leave her alone?" I asked nicely.

"Why don't *you* mind your own business?" Beverly joined in with her tribe.

"You made it my business when you started picking on my friend."

Friend? Where did that come from? The words just slipped out. I'm sure it was an accident. Patti's face lit up like a child being handed a dollar bill, and a smile flashed across her face.

"Yeah, well, your *'friend,'*" Jill seethed, fashioning her fingers into air quotes, "is spreading rumors about Sabrina."

I glanced curiously at Patti, then back to Jill.

"What kind of rumors?" I questioned.

"She said she'd heard Sabrina had been stabbed five times and that she knows who the killer is."

I felt a chill crawl down my spine. Where would Patti have heard the details about Sabrina's death? Detective Harrison didn't share that news; I'm sure he couldn't and *wouldn't*. And knowing who the killer is? How could she know something like that?

"Wait, wait, wait. Let me guess," I began in a condescending tone. "Your collective dumbasses believed her? There's no way Patti knows what happened. The police haven't released anything about her death. And do you *really* think she knows who killed Sabrina when the detective who was here doesn't even know? Use your brain."

I mean, maybe if the three of them put their heads together, it would equal *one* complete brain, but I have no data to support that theory.

"Did you just call us dumb, new girl?" Jill questioned heatedly, getting in my face, her left eye twitching. "You think you're smarter than the rest of us?"

The other two girls suddenly forgot about Patti and turned their aggressive stance toward me. I had become the *new* prey upon which the hungry vultures were eager to scavenge. Thankfully, from behind me, I felt Liza's presence.

"Is that all you girls can think about?" Liza jumped in. "Sabrina's dead, and you're all acting like a bunch of playground bullies. Do you really want to start this kind of trouble when all eyes are focused on the student body right now? How stupid can you be? Don't you get it? Sabrina's gone. Somebody killed her. We should be trying to figure out who did it instead of acting like some fucking immature preteen brats."

Wow, that was surprising. Liza always preferred to walk away from hallway drama, steering clear of those who vilified her because of her sexual orientation. Stepping into the fray so vehemently spoke volumes about her feelings for Sabrina. Jill, however, wasn't having any of it.

"Don't pretend you even care, Liza," she snapped. "It's not like you were her friend. You're probably happy she's gone. Or maybe you're just upset because it's one less girl for you to ogle, you goth freak."

That was stepping over the line. I watched Liza's nostrils flare in anger. I saw her jawbone shift through her cheeks as she clenched her teeth be-hind closed lips. I had to jump in before things got out of hand. Sabrina's friends didn't know she and Liza were an item.

"Hey, can we all just take it easy? We're all a little emotional right now because of Sabrina's mur..," I caught myself before the word came out, "because of what happened."

"Yeah," Jill responded, "*we're* the emotional ones. You didn't even know her. And as for the geek over here," she threw her thumb over her shoulder at Patti, "you'd better tell her to stop spreading her rumors and lies." She glanced back at Patti, who was cowering against a locker, and sneered. "Or maybe someone will be coming for *her* next. Let's go, girls."

The three of them turned their noses up and stomped past us, making every effort to step on Patti's homework on their way by. I shook my head at their childish behavior before turning to thank Liza.

"Thanks for stepping in like that," I said. "I was afraid there was going to be some real trouble."

"I didn't do it for you," Liza replied.

I dipped my chin sorrowfully. "I know."

Patti began picking up her books from the floor, hastily shoveling loose papers into the bind-ings, uncaring of their creased and mangled condi-tion. I bent down to lend a hand, picking up the pages closest to me.

"Patti, why would you say those things?" I questioned, handing her the papers from my squatted position. "And to *those* girls, of all people?"

"But it's true," Patti squeaked, defending her actions. "My mom called Mrs. Beaulieu to offer her condolences. She told my mom that Sabrina had been stabbed five times."

"That's awful," I responded, standing back up.

I could hear Liza starting to lose it behind me.

"What about the other part?" I asked. "Why would you say you know who did it?"

"Because," Patti said confidently. She swept up the last of the sheets of paper and stood back up. "I know who it..,"

She froze, her eyes focused over my shoulder at Liza. I peeked back and saw black tears streaming down Liza's pale cheeks. I put my arm around her and gently squeezed. I wanted her to know I was there for her. I didn't think it helped, but maybe catching Sabrina's killer would. I trained my eyes back on Patti.

"Well, go ahead, then," I urged. "Tell us who you think it was."

Patti's eyes shifted between me and Liza.

"I.., I.., gotta get to homeroom."

I don't even think the words were out of her mouth before she turned and strode away from us in a fast walk – faster than I'd ever seen her move. It was a little unusual for Patti since she always seemed to want to hang around us and outstay her welcome.

"That was weird," I said. "Since when is she in a rush to get to class?"

"I don't know," Liza said. She wiped her tears away, smudging black eyeliner across her cheeks. "And I don't care. I've got to get to class too."

She shrugged my arm from around her and walked away without so much as a 'See you later' or a 'Thank you.' Was she still bitter with me? I thought she'd be able to look past things. What the hell was wrong with everybody? Why was everyone so uptight?

Chapter 22

Broken Promises

Things were tense throughout the day. I had two classes with Liza, but she kept to herself and remained quiet the entire time. I tried reaching out to her, offering her a tender smile whenever our eyes met. She turned her head away each time. I didn't get it. What did I do that was so wrong? I've done nothing but protect and support her. She blamed me for getting Sabrina killed. That wasn't fair. All I did was invite those girls to a fake party. She was acting like I was the one who held the knife. And really, Liza could have prevented it if she'd wanted. She didn't have to go along with the scheme. She could have told her girlfriend the truth but decided not to. Why would she have done that and then act so bitter toward me as if I were the monster? She was just as much to blame.

I wonder how she would have acted if she knew what *I'd* been through this past weekend. It was a different situation, but still, I could have been killed. Then, she would have lost *me*, her best friend, and that would have been devastatingly awful. I could only hope she'd come around and talk to me again. Soon.

Until that happened, I made the most of my day. I avoided Sabrina's friends like the plague, and I managed to get out of gym class by telling Mr. Hopper I had cramps from my period. He hated hearing personal stuff like that from his students and would rather dismiss us than listen to our feminine problems. We took advantage of it any chance we could.

I wandered the halls for a bit, my thoughts divided between Sabrina's death and the whole mess with my mom and Travis. I couldn't believe things could be this bad - and just a few weeks before graduation, too. Wasn't this supposed to be the best time of my life? This whole year has been a complete nightmare. Between a bear eating my favorite teacher, moving to a new city, being questioned about a student's death, my mom killing someone, and me becoming an accomplice by helping her cover it up, I'd say it's been a year to forget. But, as I passed by the AV classroom and saw Patti sitting by herself, a miserable look on her face, I was reminded there were things I *couldn't* forget, no matter how much I fantasized about amnesia.

I opened the door just enough to poke my head inside.

"Hey, Patti. Can I come in?" Not that I waited for an answer. I needed a distraction as much as she needed company, even if she didn't want it.

Normally, Patti would have jumped with excitement, knowing someone wanted to spend time with her. Instead, she held her dour look and quietly nodded.

As I entered, I instinctively looked around, wondering if Mrs. Donaldson was nearby. She wasn't. I grabbed a chair and slid it beside Patti's, hoping her expression would change if I showed enough interest to sit as close to her as I had. She glared forward, her eyes trained on some old audio-visual equipment packed in a cardboard box on a wheeled cart. I waited a minute to see if she'd acknowledge me. It was an uncomfortable silence. I had to speak up.

"What's going on, Patti?" I asked. "You don't seem like your usual self? You're not letting those blonde bimbos' words get to you, are you?"

She turned her head and gave me a perplexed look.

"What?"

"Jill and her plastic posse," I replied. "You can't let them bother you like this."

"Oh, I don't care about them; they don't bother me."

"Oh. Then why are you looking so down?"

"It's just..," she began, struggling to get the words out. "What if you knew something bad about somebody? Would you tell anyone?"

I had to keep myself from giggling. I knew a lot of bad things about a lot of people. I had yet to tell anyone.

"Well," I responded, "how bad are we talking?"

"*Really* bad."

"In that case.., I suppose it would depend on what the consequences would be. Who needed to know? Who stood to get hurt? Was it something that could be harmful if kept a secret? There's a lot to think about."

"Okay, stop twisting my arm," Patti blurted. "I'll tell you."

Wow, I guess she couldn't hold it inside any longer.

"It was Liza!" Patti said excitedly.

"What are you talking about?" I questioned. "What was Liza?"

"I overheard her and Sabrina arguing in the bathroom after school last week. I wasn't spying on them or anything. I have bladder issues when I get anxious. Working on this stuff for graduation is really causing me problems. I couldn't hold it any longer."

"A little off track here," I stated, trying to reign her back in.

"Sorry. Anyway, I was in the bathroom when they came charging in. They didn't know I was in a stall, and after I heard their initial comments, I lifted my feet off the floor so they wouldn't see me and become embarrassed. I'd have hated that if it were me. Can you imagine? I don't even like it when..."

"Patti!" I abruptly interrupted. "Focus."

"Oh, right," she answered. "Well, they were having a very heated argument. And, well, you didn't hear this from me, but apparently, Liza and Sabrina were a couple. They were seeing each other. You know, like, in a romantic way."

I rolled my eyes at her remark. At least Patti was right about one thing; I *didn't* hear it from her, but I'd keep that to myself.

"Well, I guess they weren't anymore," Patti continued, "because Sabrina was breaking up with Liza. That's what they were fighting about. She accused Liza of smothering her too much and being too forceful. She wanted some space. Liza didn't like that and threatened her."

"Threatened her? How?"

"She told Sabrina she wouldn't let her dump her. She said if she did, she would make her pay for hurting her, for leading her on, and for playing with her feelings."

That explained why Liza hadn't warned Sabrina about the fake party. Still..,

"Okay," I responded."So they got into a fight. Stuff like that happens; it doesn't mean anything."

"Don't you see, Emma? It can't be a coincidence that Liza threatened Sabrina, and then, two days later, Sabrina ends up dead. I mean, Liza *is* a little weird. She totally seems like the type that could do something like that."

"What the hell, Patti? She's my best friend. And when has she ever said or done anything to you? Some would say *you're* a little weird, too, but you don't see us telling people *you're* the killer."

"Why would anyone think *I'm* the killer?" Patti questioned.

My words went right over her head. Of course, they did. She was so lost in her little fantasy worlds that she couldn't grasp reality. She was right, though; who would ever believe she was capable of killing someone? But Liza wasn't either. Was she?

"My point is," I replied, "people don't just kill other people because they got into an argument. That's stupid. And that's not Liza. And exactly what is a killer's 'type,' anyway?" *If she only knew my weekend.* "You know what? Nevermind."

"But..,"

"No 'buts,'" I cut her off. "I don't want to hear any more about it. Liza didn't do it."

"But..,"

"What did I just say?"

Patti dropped her head in defeat. "Okay."

"Good. Now, let's change the subject. You know that detective who was here last week?"

"That really cute one?" Patti expressed, brightening up and nodding.

Just great. Now I had to worry about Patti muscling in on my territory. Don't get any ideas; he's mine. You already have your future husband.

"That's the one," I replied. "He stopped over my house yesterday."

"What?" Why?"

Oh, how I'd love to tell her I invited him over for dinner, and that afterward, we sat on the couch and watched movies the rest of the night, holding hands and flirting with each other. That'd wipe the smile off her face.

"I think he was trying to find something where there wasn't anything to find." *Unless he decided to look in the basement*, I thought. "He asked about you, too, so you'd better figure out where you were the night of Sabrina's death."

"I was here," Patti said. "Mrs. Donaldson already vouched for me."

If only that were true. Poor Patti didn't know Detective Harrison shared what he knew with me. I should tell her, but then again, I do like secrets. And, after she accused Liza the way she had, I think I'd rather let her get out of her own mess should she be questioned again. Although, watching her stumble for an excuse now could be entertaining. No, I won't do it.

"Okay, I just thought you should know."

"Thanks, Emma."

"Sure thing," I replied.

I slapped my thighs and stood from my chair.

"I should get back to the gym. I'm sure Mr. Hopper will be thrilled to hear my 'cramps' are feeling better."

"You use that excuse, too?"

"Don't we all?"

Patti smiled.

"Take it easy, Patti. And stop letting your mind run rampant."

She nodded. "I will. Thanks for chatting with me. You're a good friend."

"Yeah." I gave her a subtle wave and walked out of the room. A good friend? I'm not so sure. Shouldn't I feel guilty for not warning her about Mrs. Donaldson changing her story? I didn't. I mean, somebody was lying. Right now, it sure looked like it was Patti. I had to wonder why. I still couldn't believe she thought Liza could hurt Sabrina. That didn't make any sense. Totally crazy.

Totally.

Crazy.

Just like Patti.

Chapter 23

Keepsake

When the last bell rang, I was out of class in a flash. I wanted to catch Liza before she left school. We hadn't talked all day, and I had to make her see I was still her friend no matter what she currently thought of me. I scrambled to her locker, hoping she'd be wedging her books into the small crevices she allotted for them, but she wasn't there. I decided to wait, thinking she'd be along at any moment. What I hadn't planned on was Jill and her latest sucker.., I mean, boyfriend, and the other two blonde stooges, to come barreling down the hallway with their figurative pitchforks and torches in hand. They were on a witch hunt. Apparently, I was the one wearing the black, pointy hat. They surrounded me, keeping my back against the lockers. A crowd of curious gawkers filled the hall, gathered to bear witness to the stake-burning ceremony.

"I hear you've been causing trouble with my girlfriend," the brainless jock said. He put his arm around Jill's shoulders, an arrogant look on his face. She batted her eyelashes and flashed him a smile even a seasoned actress would be proud of, then turned and glared at me with a cocky smirk.

"Let me guess, Jason. Your little princess got her feelings hurt and asked you to make her feel all better? Are you here to convince me to stop picking on her, or are you here to beat up on poor, defenseless me?"

"I don't hit girls," he said.

Such a gentleman.

"I won't even make an exception for a freak like you," he added.

That's it; I'm taking back that "gentleman" thought.

"So then, why are you even here?" I questioned.

"Just because I don't hit girls doesn't mean I can't make your life miserable. Isn't that right, babe?" He glanced down at Jill, who pressed her cheek against his shoulder and placed her hand on the center of his chest.

"That's right, my big, strong grizzly bear." She gave him a quick peck on the lips while keeping her eyes sideways on me to catch my reaction.

Was this what Jason meant? Because right now, this little scene *was* making me miserable.

And a touch nauseous. I think it was time to give up one of my secrets. I hated to do it, but the situation demanded it.

"I'm so sorry you feel that way, Jason," I began. "But it's so good to see you still appreciate Jill after all the hoops she made you jump through."

"What are you talking about?" Jason asked.

"Yeah, Emma," Jill jumped in. "What are you talking about?"

"Oh, come on, Jill. There's no need to pretend." I turned my attention to Jason. "It must have been so humiliating when she told you she wanted to watch you have sex with one of her stuffed animals before she would let you stick your penis in her."

I watched Jason's eyes widen, his face become flush.

"Let me ask you – did she cut the hole in it or did you?" I added. "I hope you didn't go through with it."

Jill's jaw dropped. The gathered students began snickering and pointing. Even Trina and Beverly took a step back and gave Jill a confused look. Jason dropped his arm from Jill's shoulder and gritted his teeth.

"Oh my God, Jill," he seethed. "You said you wouldn't tell anyone."

"But I didn't," she replied, reaching for his hands.

He sharply pulled them away. "You lying bitch. I can't believe you. I should have known you were nothing but a warped little slut."

"Jason, I..,

Jill's pleading stopped when Jason abruptly shoved her aside and weaved his way through the crowd of laughing on-lookers.

"The stuffed animal was better than you any-way, you skanky bitch!" he yelled out over the horde, no doubt a last-ditch effort to save face with his peers.

It didn't surprise me how upset Jill seemed when she turned her lasered stare back to me. I must have had such a victorious grin on my face. It served her right for trying to sic her "grizzly bear" on me. She balled her hands into fists and thrust them downward at her sides.

"Ooh," she grumbled through clenched teeth. "How could you do that to me? You cost me a per-fectly good boyfriend."

"You brought it on yourself," I replied. "You couldn't let it go."

"You're really pushing my buttons, Emma."

"Only pushing?" I responded. "Darn - I'm try-ing to *punch* your buttons."

"You're such a bitch." She turned and started walking away. "Come on, girls."

Trina and Beverly looked at each other, won-dering who would take the first step. Neither made a forward move. When Jill realized her teammates hadn't catered to her demand, she curled her upper lip.

"Whatever, losers."

As Jill continued her walk of shame, the rest of the students taunted her with shouts of Teddy bears and stuffed unicorns. Trina and Beverly didn't join in, choosing to back away and quietly vanish in the opposite direction. I think Jill lost more than her boyfriend. She never had dignity, so it wasn't that.

That was the power of secrets. They could save people, or they could destroy them. Jason thought Jill had betrayed him, divulging a secret they both shared. That couldn't have been further from the truth. Jill didn't want that secret getting out, either. Nope, that was Scott Chauncy's doing.

Scott was a junior on the debate team that Jill toyed with for a couple of weeks before she broke it off with him. He was constantly writing things in his notebook. He barely ever took the time to look up from the pages. We always thought he was diligently preparing for his next debate. It was too bad he left school in a hurry one day and forgot his notebook. Well, too bad for him, anyway. I was okay with it since I sat next to him in class.

Scott's house was on my way home, and, being the perfectly innocent student I am, I decided to bring it to him. As it turned out, while I perused through the pages, there wasn't anything even remotely related to debating subjects. It was an odd collection of personal stories and intimate reflections on his daily life, including an interestingly detailed section about his relationship with Jill. I specifically took note of the part where Jill asked Scott to have sex with a stuffed giraffe she kept on a chair by her bed. When he balked at the idea, she told him he wasn't the only one; every guy she'd ever been with had done it with one of her animals. After hearing that, the dumb, sex-starved kid reluctantly succumbed to her request. Honestly, who could blame him? After all, his reward was Jill. She might be a stuck-up snob, but to a hormonally-charged teenage boy, she was still a fine piece of ass.

Sure, it could have been a one-time thing. Maybe Jill lied to him about all the other guys doing it. But if you read his detailed notes about how turned-on Jill had become when he ravaged that poor, cotton-stuffed creature and how she had dozens of stuffed animals around her room (all with smiles on their faces, I'd bet), her strange sexual fetish rang of gross truth. I took a gamble; it paid off. Teenage boys were so easily played.

With the afternoon's entertainment now over, the rest of the students dispersed with shameless smiles still glued to their faces. Some of them gave me a thumbs-up on their way by - as if their seal of approval meant something to me. Don't get me wrong; it did, more than I'd let on, but, at the moment, the more important thing was getting my friend back.

Why won't you talk to me, Liza?

Chapter 24

Sliver

I thought long and hard about swinging by Liza's house after school. I needed to clear the air between us. She was my best friend – my *only* friend since my mom and I moved here. I know; sad. People here hadn't warmed up to me like at my previous school. Anyway, I decided against it. I didn't think Liza's mother would like someone showing up out of the blue, and the last thing I wanted was for Liza to get in trouble for something I did. That would only make things worse between us.

I decided to walk home instead. There were plenty of other things in my screwed-up existence that needed fixing. I couldn't dwell on a broken friendship when my mom was all stressed out from killing her ex-boyfriend. Honestly, I was surprised at how well *I* was handling the whole murder/hiding the dead body situation. What a change from when we first moved here.

Back then, I thought my mom was a rock. After everything that had happened to her - the abuse, the rumors about everything that was going on at the school, the job relocation, she was as steady as Gibraltar. I, on the other hand, was a wreck. I'd lost my home, my friends, my favorite teacher, everything. Even so, I thought it'd be easy for me to fit in since I was so well-liked, but the students were different here at Bellamy.

I remember coming home on more than one occasion, almost in tears, venting to my mom about the students being so mean to me. Mean isn't the right word. They were oblivious to me. It was always about those cheerleaders. It wasn't that they had said or done anything in a way to hurt me (not all of them, anyway). I could have handled that. It was just that they were so damn popular. That used to be me at my last school. *I* was the popular one. Here, people didn't notice me. I hated them for that. I had Liza and nobody else. My poor mom took the brunt of all my frustrations and talked me down from the ledge. She made me realize it would take time for others to come around. *"Good things come to those who wait,"* she would tell me. Unfortunately, I was still waiting.

I'd developed thicker skin since then. It was now *my* turn to be the rock for my mom. She was acting strong, trying to keep it together for my sake, but I could tell she was a sliver away from losing it. I couldn't let that happen. If she slipped up, we were both going down.

I was so wrapped up in my thoughts that I didn't hear the car approaching from behind until I heard the brakes squeal, bringing it to a stop at the edge of the sidewalk beside me.

"Hello, Emma."

I ducked my head a bit to see who the driver was, even though the voice and the car gave it away.

"Detective Harrison? Are you following me?"

A girl could only hope.

"Haha," he chuckled, displaying his perfect, white teeth, obscured slightly behind perfect lips and that perfectly formed smile. "That doesn't sound like me."

Rats!

"No, I just left the Beaulieu residence and am headed back to the station."

"You were at Sabrina's house?" I questioned. "How are her parents doing?"

"They're holding it together the best they can under the circumstances. I try to keep them informed about the investigation."

"About that," I said. "Can I ask you a question?"

"Shoot."

"Was Sabrina stabbed to death?"

His smile faded.

"I'm sorry, Emma, I can't discuss details about the case. I'm curious, however; why do you ask?"

"Rumors are spreading around school that that's what happened. I watch a lot of true crime shows, and it got me thinking - if that were true, isn't stabbing someone usually considered to be a crime of passion? It seems, in most cases, it turns out to be a spouse or partner."

"*If* that were true," he replied, "and I'm not saying it is, then stabbing someone is typically more personal, yes. But, even so, we've already confirmed Sabrina's boyfriend was working that night."

"Right," I said, nodding. "Not the boyfriend. Did you check her texts?"

The detective looked at me curiously. "We did. Unfortunately, we found her phone smashed and the sim card missing. Her data carrier only stores messages for five days, so there was limited information. Why do I get the feeling you're not telling me something? Is there something you know that I'm missing?"

"Me? No!" I immediately replied. "I just think it's horrible what happened. We all want justice for Sabrina."

"It *is* horrible," he responded. "And we appreciate everyone's cooperation in this. I know Sabrina's death has affected a lot of the students, but it doesn't do any good to speculate. That only adds to the rumors that are already spreading. Leave the detective work to the professionals."

"Got it."

Detective Harrison glanced forward, then back at me.

"Can I give you a ride home?" he asked. "I'm driving right by your street."

Oh, you can give me a ride, all right, I thought. *Should we hop in the backseat now?*

"Now, Detective Harrison," I began, "what would Mrs. Harrison think if she knew you were picking up a girl from the side of the road?"

"If there *were* a Mrs. Harrison," he answered, "I'm sure she'd appreciate that I was looking out for the safety of the city's residents by offering a ride."

I was sure he rambled off a bunch of words, but I didn't hear anything past "*If there were a Mrs. Harrison.*" Handsome *and* single. If I accepted the ride, who knew where it would lead? That could be fun. Or dangerous. It was best if I kept walking.

"Thanks, Detective, but it's such a nice day out, I think I'll walk."

"Very well," he replied.

I thought he was going to drive off when he saw me starting to walk again, but instead, he shouted out the passenger window, grabbing my attention.

"Oh, hey. I noticed your uncle decided not to head back home just yet."

"What?" I questioned.

"I saw his car at the Big W Superstore earlier today. I couldn't mistake that beauty."

"Oh, right," I replied. "Yeah, he decided to stay another week."

"Well, good. I hope that means he's enjoying the area."

"He is," I said, staring off into the distance like I was anxious to end the conversation.

Detective Harrison took the hint. "All right then," he said, putting his hand up in a subtle wave. "I'll let you get on back home."

"Thank you. Goodbye."

"Bye, Emma."

He drove off, leaving me frozen in place. Did I say I was a rock? Maybe I should rethink that. I could feel my knees shaking and my breath becoming shallow.

"Shit, shit," I whispered to myself. "I've got to do something about the car."

Chapter 25

Thorns

If you looked closely enough, you could almost see another strip of gray growing from my mom's scalp right before your eyes. This latest one was brought on by my upsetting news that Travis' high-profile Camaro needed to be moved from its current location. It already attracted Detective Harrison's attention and would look even more suspicious if it remained.

"It can't stay there," I said.

My mom's shoulders fell in disappointment.

"We'll have to bring it back here," I continued.

"I don't want that car in my driveway," my mom argued. "You said it'd be safe to leave it in that parking lot."

She was getting upset – understandably so. I'd told her everything was going to work out. It was my idea to park it in a public space, and now I was changing my tune. Sure, it was risky, leaving a murder victim's vehicle at our house, but our options were limited. My original plan wouldn't have been an issue if Travis drove a Nissan Altima or a Toyota Rav4 like regular people. It would have easily blended in with the sea of bland-looking cars. But no. He just had to be a special kind of narcissist and get himself a fancy muscle car. He was probably making up for other inadequacies.

"I know, but we can't," I fired back. "I don't like the idea of bringing it back here, either, Mom, but we have no choice. The detective who stopped by yesterday already noticed it and asked me about it. I made up a story, but now, it's gotta come back - at least, until we can figure out something else to do with it."

"What *are* we going to do with it?" she yelled. "This isn't right. I should tell the police what I did."

"Mom, no!" I belted. "You'll go to jail. And for what? Over Travis? He was a dirtbag who tried to kill you. You can't go to the police. I don't want to lose you."

"I don't know if I can do this, Emma."

"You can," I assured her. "You have to. I'll figure something out. Just.., please.., trust me on this."

She rubbed her forehead and began pacing about the living room. I didn't know what to say to make things better. But fate certainly knew how to make things worse as, just then, my phone vibrated. I never should have taken it out of my back pocket, but I thought it was Liza finally reaching out to me. Boy, that was a wrong assumption.

It won't be long until everyone finds out.

"Shit. I can't deal with this right now."

I didn't even realize I said it out loud until my mom stopped her pacing and glared at me.

"Honey, no one can deal with this."

"It's not that, Mom," I snapped before thinking. "It's these stupid texts." Crap – I didn't mean to let that out, either.

"What texts?" she questioned. "Who is that?"

"It's nothing, nobody," I replied. "Don't worry about it."

She saw right through my blatant lie.

"It didn't sound like 'nothing.' And with everything else that's going on, how can I *not* worry about it? Is it about the car?"

"Mom, stop!"

"Emma, this is the second time I've seen that look," she pressed. "You had the same nervous expression when you received a text during the detective's visit yesterday. Is it the same person?"

"Mom! Leave it be. I'll handle it."

She exhaled heavily. "You asked me to trust you, Emma; now, I'm asking *you*. Who texted you just now?"

I hated when she got like this. She wasn't going to stop nagging until I told her.

"I don't know," I said.

"What do you mean you don't know?"

"I mean, I don't know. It's from an unknown number."

"Well, what's it say?" she prodded.

I couldn't be upset with her for prying. It was my own fault. I was usually better at controlling my emotions. I slipped up. And because of it, I now had to *fess* up. Another secret ripped from me.

I handed her my phone with the messages displayed. She scrolled through the small handful, then tilted her head up.

"What does all this mean?" she asked. "What did you do?"

"I didn't do anything," I replied.

"Did you tell anyone about Travis? Is that what this is about?"

"No, Mom," I argued. "Look at the dates. Most of them came in before Travis was even here."

"Then, what's it about?" she questioned. She held the phone up to me, shoulder-height, and pointed to the screen.

"I told you, I don't know."

"Well, I'm going to find out."

Before I could react, my mom began typing away.

"Mom, what are you doing?" I swung my arm forward to snatch the phone from her, but she turned away, determined to get her words in.

"There; now we'll see what they have to say."

She handed me my phone, and I nervously looked to see what she typed.

```
Whoever you are, you have the wrong number.
Keep this up, and you'll be in a world of
shit.
```

"Mom!" I exclaimed. "What the hell?"

"What?"

"'You'll be in a world of shit'? Really?"

"Someone is obviously playing a prank on you," she responded. "Sometimes you gotta put a little scare into these people to make them stop."

No sooner did her words come out than my phone blew up.

```
Wrong number? I don't think so.
Was that a threat?
What are you going to do?
Kill me?
I bet that would make you happy.
Maybe you think this is all a joke.
But what you did wasn't a joke.
And soon, you'll pay.
You'll pay for it all.
```

Chapter 26
The Color Red

Way to go, Mom. I shared one secret with you, and you had to twist the knife. Whoever was on the other end of that line wasn't happy. And I still had no idea what they were talking about. Maybe my mom was right; someone was playing a joke on me. It didn't feel like a joke. Whoever it was, they blamed me for something, and they weren't about to back down despite my mom's best effort to scare them. If anything, she ramped them up. Just what I needed on top of everything else: someone with a misguided vendetta.

It didn't do me any good to worry about someone who obviously mistook me for someone else. I had too many other things going on that needed my attention. The first of which was Travis' car.

It took the entire trip to convince my mom, but she finally realized this was the only way. We had to bring the car back to our house. Thankfully, it was only a temporary situation.

"Just stop here, Mom," I said as we approached the Camaro. "I'll get it and follow you back home."

"Are you sure you don't want me driving it instead?" she asked. "What if you get pulled over?"

"I'll be fine, Mom," I said as I opened the door to get out. "Just drive the speed limit so I don't get any ideas."

I gave her a playful grin. In return, she shook her head and gave me a stern look.

"Not funny," she said.

"Sure it was," I replied. Then, I tucked my hair up under my old softball cap and closed the door.

All right, I'll admit it. Getting to drive the Camaro was pretty cool. It had some horsepower under the hood, and if I didn't play it cautiously by following behind my mom, the temptation to see what that baby could do might be too great. No.., driving at my mom's snail's pace would be the best bet. It wouldn't be all bad, though. Even driving slow, I was sure I looked damn hot to anyone who saw me behind the wheel.

My mom pulled forward, giving me just enough room to back out. I thought she'd go ahead and turn down the next row, but I guess she figured I needed to follow her through the parking lot instead of meeting her at the exit. Older people were funny.

On the drive home, I started thinking about what Patti had told me. As if driving a dead man's car wasn't bad enough, I had to deal with the conspiracy theory she'd concocted. Until I calmed her down, she was convinced Liza had something to do with Sabrina's death because she overheard an argument between the two of them. That was ridiculous. Why was Patti so quick to want to throw Liza under the bus like that? It was a crazy assumption. People argue. It didn't mean someone was going to end up dead. Although, in this case, somebody *did* end up dead. But that didn't mean it was Liza who killed her. And Patti shouldn't have been thinking that it was. Liza has been nothing but a friend to her. We both have. The whole thing was nonsense.

Right. If I believed that, why was it still lingering in my thoughts? Could it be a coincidence that Sabrina ended up dead soon after she told Liza she was breaking up with her? What am I thinking? Of course, it was a coincidence. Why am I letting Patti's words get to me? Although, if Patti heard correctly, Liza *did* threaten Sabrina. I didn't think Liza was like that. Then again, I also didn't think Liza would keep any secrets from me, but clearly, I was wrong about that. Her relationship with Sabrina caught me off guard. Maybe I didn't know her as well as I thought.

And what about Patti? How well did I know her? Maybe she was lying about what she overheard. After all, I'd already caught her in a lie, though she didn't know it. She wasn't with Mrs. Donaldson the night of Sabrina's murder. Why did she lie about that? What was she trying to hide? Could she have killed Sabrina and was now trying to pin it on Liza? Why would she do that? It didn't make sense.

Who was I kidding? None of this made sense. Why was I automatically singling out someone from my school? This wasn't one of those soap operas my mom used to watch, where everything bad that happened revolved around your closest circle of friends. Not everyone was hiding something dark. It was more likely that Sabrina was killed by some rando who was looking for a good time, and when she wouldn't give him what he wanted, he killed her. But, there *was* the matter of the soda bottle at the scene – with mine and Patti's fingerprints all over it. How did that get there? Some random person wouldn't have had it. And the police and that hottie detective wouldn't be questioning the students the way they were unless they felt there was somehow a connection. Huh. Maybe real life was more like a soap opera than I realized.

My thoughts quickly snapped back to the current problem as I followed my mom's car onto our street. I grabbed my phone to dial her number and noticed a text had come through. It was from Liza.

```
I'm sorry I've been acting so weird lately.
I need to talk to someone. Can we meet up?
```

I felt relief wash over me. I thought I'd lost Liza forever. We were graduating in three weeks, and who knew where our lives would take us after that? If I never saw Liza again, would I ever feel good about how we left things? I needed her back in my life. I needed to clear the air and make her see it wasn't my fault. But not before I straightened out this whole car mess.

I dialed my mom.

"I see you holding the phone, young lady," she answered. "You should have both hands on the wheel."

"Really, Mom? That's what you're going to focus on?"

She wasn't so concerned last night when I was transporting her dead ex-boyfriend. The woman was getting loopy. I didn't think she was handling things well. We needed to sit down and talk – get things out. It would do us both some good.

"Let me pull in first," I said.

"Right," she answered. "We'll need my car available."

"Yup. Bye."

Although that was true, my first thought was to hide the car from sight the best we could. I thought about removing the license plates, but that would look suspicious. I'm now starting to under-stand why the bad guys in the movies always deserted the car on a dirt road. It was hard to think of everything.

My mom pulled to the side of the road just before our yard to let me pass. I pulled into the driveway, and she followed suit, leaving enough room to access the Camaro's trunk. Right, the blanket and cardboard. Good thinking, Mom.

I didn't get out right away. We were home. We were safe (if there was such a thing). I closed my eyes and leaned my head back against the headrest. I drew in a breath and let it out. I could have sat there for an hour, letting my thoughts settle down, if not for my mom's voice disturbing the quiet as she walked by the window.

"Are you coming?" she asked. "I don't want you in that car longer than you need to be."

I nodded. "I'm just going to grab the blanket and cardboard from the trunk."

"Oh, right - the cardboard and blanket," she replied.

So much for giving her credit for leaving room between the vehicles; she didn't even remember. She walked in the front door, and I reached for my phone.

```
Of course, we can meet. Where? When?
```

While I waited for Liza's reply, I stepped from the vehicle, and the idea hit me like a freight train.

A car cover.

Why didn't I think of that before? It would have been so easy. We could have covered the car, and nobody would have thought twice about it. How could I have not thought of that? Oh, I don't know.., maybe because I was too busy thinking about disposing of a bloody corpse? Whatever. It was too late now. Detective Harrison already saw the car. If, for whatever reason, he stopped over again, it wouldn't make sense for it to be covered. My "uncle" was only here for another week. Lesson learned. If ever I find myself having to get rid of another dead body and having to hide the person's vehicle, a car cover will be my first thought.

I grabbed the stuff from the trunk, rolling up the blanket into a messy ball, and tucked it under one arm while I held the cardboard by one of the hand slots I'd cut into it. It was time to burn them. Throwing them in the fire pit out back would eliminate two more pieces of evidence that could link my mom to any crime. Damn, that was something a daughter should never have to think.

I hauled the DNA-riddled things out back and threw them into the bricked-out circle filled with charred ash. It dawned on me we hadn't sat out here in front of a fire in months. Maybe now was the best time. We needed to talk. What better way than to do it over the burning remnants of a past we both needed to forget?

I ran inside to grab a lighter and convinced my mom to join me. She was reluctant at first, but I was persuasive. Okay, if you must know, I guilted her into it. Hey, I never said I was an angel. Even if my mom believed I was.

I lit the fire, and we sat and watched the flame spread over the blanket, the red-stained blotches turning black before disintegrating into floating debris carried upward and away on the evening's subtle breeze. I glanced over at my mom, her face showing little emotion in the flickering light of the flame as she stared blankly at the growing fire. She was lost in her thoughts and sinking deeper. She wouldn't like it, but it was time for that talk.

"Mom."

She lifted her eyes and chin from the fire pit, her expression that of someone who had just been snapped out of a trance - like she'd forgotten I was across from her until she heard my voice.

"What is it, Emma?"

Just then, my phone buzzed on my lap. I looked at the screen.

```
Tonight. In an hour. The old mill building
where..., well, you know.
```

Shit. So much for that talk.

"What did you want, honey?" she asked.

"Can I get a ride into town?"

Chapter 27

No Sympathy

On the ride into town, it wasn't exactly the talk I had hoped for, but there *were* spoken words. That had to count for something.

"You're not acting like yourself," I said.

"What are you talking about?" My mom answered.

"I'm talking about your emotional state."

"There's nothing wrong with my emotional state."

"Okay, Mom," I said sarcastically, forming my thumb and index finger into a circle to display an "OK" sign. "You've been up, you've been down; I feel like you're playing out lyrics to a Katy Perry song."

"What's wrong with Katy Perry?"

"That's not the point. You've been through an ordeal – we both have, and you need to let it out."

"Let what out?"

"Whatever is going on inside your head. You can't keep it bottled up. It's okay to talk about it with me. I'm not a little girl anymore."

"Honey, you're being ridiculous. There's nothing wrong with me."

"But Mom..,"

"Emma!" she shouted. "That's enough! Just because you want something to be true doesn't mean it is. I'm fine."

I bit my lip and stared out my side window. Silence took over the next few moments. I could see in my window's reflection my mom kept turning her head to me every few seconds. I think she felt bad for yelling at me.

"Are *you?*" my mom questioned.

"Am I what?" I snapped, continuing to look out my window in frustrated defiance.

"Are you fine?"

"It's not me you have to worry about," I responded.

"Well, I do worry about you. I'll always worry."

"Mom," I turned to look at her, "you killed a man. Brutally. Then we both covered it up. We're both dealing with some shit. You ask me if I'm fine. Well, I'm not. Okay? But at least I'm not afraid to admit it. Or even talk about it."

Another stretch of silence swept in and captured the moment. My mom stared forward out the windshield, guilt prominently displayed on her face. Her hands were gripped tightly on the steering wheel at ten and two.

"I'm sorry you got caught up in all of that," she said without breaking her focus from the road. "When I saw Travis put his hands on you, something inside me snapped. I couldn't let him hurt you. I couldn't let him hurt anyone else. I didn't know what I was doing; I just reacted. Yes, I killed someone. But he wasn't a man. A man wouldn't treat women the way he did. And if I had it to do over again, and he laid his hands on you, I'd kill him again. He doesn't deserve my sympathy. So, if you think I'm acting weird, then I don't want to act normal. You're my daughter, and I'd do anything to protect you."

I saw a single tear escape from my mom's right eye and watched it slowly trickle down her cheek. I reached forward and placed my hand on hers. She turned and smiled, fighting to keep more tears from falling. Was this a moment? Were we having a moment? I've read about such things and seen them on television. I thought it was all fake for dramatic purposes, yet here we were, starring in our own Lifetime movie.

Get ahold of yourself, Emma, I thought. *This sappy emotional stuff isn't you.* I quickly pulled my hand away from hers and adjusted myself in my seat. I couldn't let this.., whatever "this" was, affect me. Thankfully, the timing worked out perfectly. "You can drop me off here, Mom."

Chapter 28

Messed Up

I had my mom drop me off at the plaza down-town. I couldn't tell her my real plan, the place where Liza had asked me to meet her. That would have gone over like a fart in church. I could picture it now.

"Hey, Mom, can you drop me off at the old mill building? Liza wants to meet up there."

"Isn't that where Sabrina was found dead?"

"Yeah."

"You're grounded for life. Go to your room."

That sounded about right. Whatever; it was fine. The old mill was within walking distance from the plaza. The walk would do me some good and give me a chance to think things through.

Although I was relieved to see Liza's text come through - I've been wanting to patch things up between us - it was weird, and maybe a little creepy, that she wanted to meet at the old mill building. The police must have had that place cordoned off with police tape. Maybe she's seeking closure. Maybe Liza needed to see where her girlfriend died so she could get past it, and she wanted me there for moral support. It all sounded reasonable. Sure, let's go with that. It made total sense.

Of course, there could be a far darker reason. What if Patti was right, and Liza killed Sabrina? What if she planned to make me her next victim to keep me from talking? After all, as far as Liza was concerned, I was the only person who knew about her and Sabrina's relationship. Shit! Maybe I should forget about all this, call my mom, and have her pick me up. No. Stop it, Emma. You're becoming paranoid. You *know* Liza. You know she couldn't do something like that. Have a little faith in your best friend.

Damn you, Patti! Why did you have to put those thoughts in my head?

At least it was a warm night. The air was calm. Not enough to calm me, though. It was getting dark; there weren't a lot of people out. Fewer people meant fewer eyes watching me cut down the service road toward the old abandoned factories. Was that a good or bad thing? Only time would tell if I'd wished there were witnesses to my whereabouts. I didn't want to become the next subject of the gossipmongers at my school.

"Emma was the best student this school ever had," the teachers would brag about me after the police found my body.

"And she was so pretty and intelligent," the students would praise.

Oh yeah, real intelligent. I'm so smart that I agreed to sneak into a crime scene to meet with someone who could very well be the murderer in the murder investigation. It made all the sense in the world. And worse, Liza wasn't even on the police's radar. Instead, it was me and Patti who looked like their suspects. It was all messed up. The whole thing would almost be funny if it weren't so freaking crazy.

As I came around the bend, I saw Liza waiting by the chainlink fence out front, and a sudden feeling of relief washed over me. I was worried I was going to have to find a way inside the building and have to look for her in the dark. She was carrying a backpack, which she slipped off her shoulders and rested at her feet as I approached.

"Liza, what are we doing here?" I asked in almost a whisper, though I didn't know why since there wasn't anyone around.

"I need your help," she replied.

"Why? What's going on?"

Liza looked around suspiciously as if she was worried I'd been followed. She began scratching her arm nervously like she was a heroin addict aching for her next fix.

"I'm kinda freaking out here," she said.

"I can tell," I responded. "And you're going to start freaking *me* out because of it."

"I'm sorry. It's just..,"

She became silent, struggling with something.

"What is it, Liza? It's me. You can tell me."

She gave me a regretful look, then reached down and unzipped her pack. I'd be lying if I said that didn't make me nervous. Was she digging for a weapon? Was this it? Was this where I would meet my end – at an abandoned factory with nobody around to hear me scream or gasp my final breath? That would be a real bummer. When she stood back up, I reacted to my self-induced fears and backed away. She was holding two flashlights in her hand. I felt relieved and stupid at the same time. She held one out for me.

"I need help finding something," Liza said.

I grabbed the flashlight she offered. "Okay. What?"

"Promise me you won't say anything to anybody."

Ooohh! A secret! I liked where this was going.

"I won't tell anyone. I promise."

She hesitated. I stared into her eyes and reassured her.

"Liza, I promise."

She dropped her chin to her chest and exhaled heavily.

"We need to find a knife."

"The *killer's* knife?" I questioned, a bit more vocal than I had intended since it caught me off guard.

"*My* knife," she said.

At her reply, I felt my knees buckle; my chest tightened. I thought my heart stopped for a moment.

"What do you mean, your knife?" I questioned, my voice quivering. "Liza, did..,"

I paused, wondering how to ask what I was afraid to ask. There was no time for subtleties. I just had to go for it and hoped I'd see another day.

"Did you kill Sabrina? I don't know if I could handle that."

"No, I didn't kill her! How could you think that?"

"You just told me we're looking for your knife. At a murder scene where a girl was stabbed to death. What am I *supposed* to think?"

"Not that I killed her," she replied.

"Then what?" I responded. "Explain it to me. What the hell is going on here?"

"Okay, I will, but.., don't freak out."

"Too late for that."

"It's not what you think."

"Then tell me."

"I was here the night of the fake party," she began. "I didn't tell you because I didn't want you to know about me and Sabrina. I texted her that day after school to let her know there was no party. I told her not to tell the others because I wanted to meet with her to talk, and Jill was her only ride. We had gotten into an argument a few days before, and I wanted to work things out between us."

"So you brought a knife with you?" I interjected. "What were you going to do? Threaten her to continue seeing you?"

"What? No! I brought it with me for protection, Emma. I was going to an abandoned building alone and at night. I didn't know if there would be squatters, or drug dealers, or rapists out here. And I wasn't going to take the chance. So I took a knife with me.

"I got here a little early to scope things out. I wanted to make sure things were safe. I found a door on the side that somebody had already pried open, and so I waited inside."

I threw my hands up and gave her a questioning look. "And you didn't think maybe somebody was already inside?"

"Duh. I'm not stupid. I called out first; nobody answered."

I shook my head. "Oh, right, then it must've been safe. A raving lunatic would never think to keep quiet when hiding out in a creepy abandoned building."

Liza tilted her head sideways and gave me a snarky look. "Are you done?"

"Sorry," I replied. "Go on."

"Sabrina texted me to keep me updated," Liza continued. "Knowing the other girls would want to leave right away after finding the place deserted,

Sabrina said she would ask Jill to drop her off at the diner down the street where her mom works and that she would catch a ride home with her."

"Okay. Sabrina gets dropped off and walks back here. And, so, what? You guys just talked?" I asked.

"More like fought," she replied.

"You're not helping your case," I responded.

"Stop it, Emma! I told you I didn't do anything. I just wanted her to hear what I had to say, but she wouldn't listen to me. She kept telling me it was a mistake we'd gotten together. That I wasn't someone she could see herself with. When I tried to tell her how much I loved her, she yelled at me and told me to grow up. Then she whipped out her phone and told me she was deleting me from her contacts and wiping all our text messages away. I begged her not to, but she did it right in front of me and said, 'There. It's like you never existed to me.' I was so hurt; I could feel myself about to cry. But I wasn't going to let her see me that way. I couldn't. So, I ran out as fast as I could but ended up doing something stupid. I tripped outside the door and fell flat on my face. That's when I heard Sabrina laughing at me. I never thought she could be so cruel. I stood up, dusted myself off, and continued running until I got home.

"Later, when I went to take the knife out of my jacket pocket, it was gone. I must've lost it when I fell."

"And you think it's somewhere out here?"

"It has to be."

"All right, but If you didn't kill Sabrina, what are you so worried about?"

"It has my prints on it. If the police find the knife, they'll know I was here."

"So. You can explain to them what you just told me."

"Ha! If I can't get my best friend to believe me, how do you suppose I'd convince the police?"

"Liza, I.., I believe you."

Do I? Or is it just that I *want* to?

"Well, let's get looking, then," I said. "If you did drop it here, it's got to be close by. What's it look like?"

"I don't know; it looks like a knife."

"That's a big help. Is it long or short? Does it fold up like a Swiss army knife?"

"It doesn't fold up; it's a kitchen knife. It's medium-sized and has a black handle with a gold-colored ring around it."

"You see, now that's what you should have led with," I responded.

"Are you going to keep talking, or are you going to help look?"

"I'm looking, I'm looking."

We searched the area for about twenty minutes, kicking aside leaves and digging through the scoured-about litter that people had uncaringly discarded over the years. I kept looking over at the doorway Liza had crept into that night. The door was slightly ajar, but there was still yellow police tape crisscrossed over the entryway. I didn't dare go inside, but I did pause to shine a light into the opening.

"What about the soda bottle?" I asked.

"The what?"

"The police found a soda bottle at the scene. Did you bring it?"

"No. But I do remember seeing one inside while I was waiting for Sabrina. What does that have to do with anything?"

That was a secret I'd like to keep for now.

"Nothing," I replied. I turned from the doorway and flashed the light in a wide swath across the area we'd already searched. "I don't think you lost it here. Unless..,"

"'Unless,' what?"

"Oh, nothing," I answered. "I just don't think you lost it here."

How could I tell her the "unless" part? How could I tell her that she must not have lost it here *unless* she did, and someone found it and used it to kill Sabrina? In a way, that would mean Sabrina's death was kinda Liza's fault. That would devastate her. I wouldn't do that to her. She'd been through enough. We all had. It was time to let this be and go home.

"Maybe it bounced out of your pocket on your run home," I said. "It could be anywhere."

Liza circled the flashlight around her in desperation. It was no use.

"Come on, Liza. It's not here. Let's get out of here before we get caught. We wouldn't be able to explain *that*."

She looked at me pitifully, and I nudged my head sideways toward the access road. She was reluctant to leave, but she also knew I was right. We couldn't stay here, and there was nothing to find. She conceded, and we both walked away, our heads drooped low. I had so many thoughts swirling in my head, as I'm sure she did, too, but neither of us was willing to give them up.

We got to the main road and said our goodbyes like we were strangers passing in the night. She went her way; I went mine. I knew there would be more conversations to come. I wasn't sure how I felt about that. If Liza was lying, she could be the killer. If she was telling the truth, then someone else was at the building before she arrived – someone who left the conspicuous soda bottle lying around with mine and Patti's fingerprints on it.

I had questions. One way or another, I was going to get some answers. I just hoped I wouldn't regret what I found out. As if *that* ever happened.

Chapter 29

The Hits Keep Coming

My fixed stare out the windshield was purposeful. I wanted to avoid unnecessary eye contact. Sure, my mom was a little off, but she was with it enough to tell when something was gnawing at me. Whatever outward appearances I confidently portrayed to my friends, my classmates, or even my teachers.., none of them worked on my mom. She could always see through the phony façade. No, it was best not to let her see it at all. The darkness was my friend, and though the center console's dim light strained to unveil what I'd rather stay hidden, it wasn't enough to expose the darker feeling churning within.

"Did you have a good time with your friend?" my mom asked, breaking the silence that had occupied the vehicle since she picked me up.

"It was okay," I replied, keeping my head forward. I kept my answer short and sweet, hoping she wouldn't ask me to elaborate. I reached forward to turn on the radio to discourage further questioning when she stopped me by placing her hand over the knob.

"Now, hold on," she said. "Aren't you going to tell me about it? What did you guys do? Did you eat?"

"Mom, we didn't do anything; we just hung out and talked, okay?"

"Okay," she replied, taking her hand away from the dash and throwing it up defensively. "I was just making conversation."

"Well, you don't have to," I said, pressing the power button on the radio.

Nirvana's Lithium sounded out, swallowing any chance of renewed talking before it began. I bobbed my head to the music while staring out my side window, watching the mailboxes streak by. The lyrics were playing, but my thoughts were in a different place. I couldn't stop thinking about Liza being at the old mill the night of Sabrina's death. And that she had a knife with her, too. She said she didn't kill her. I wanted to believe that was true, but I kept hearing my mom's words ring out, *"Just because you want something to be true doesn't mean it is."* But it *was* true; it had to be. I had to believe Liza couldn't.., no.., she *wouldn't* kill anybody. I was sure of it.

And then there's the matter of the soda bottle. If Liza didn't bring it, then who did? She said it was inside when she got there. Was she playing me? Did she kill Sabrina and then leave the soda bottle to steer suspicion away from her and toward me and Patti? Why would she do that?

So much for being sure Liza wouldn't kill anybody. I was already condemning her before I knew anything. What kind of best friend was I? Oh, wait, I know this one - the kind that helps look for a knife at a crime scene. What was I thinking?

Right. This was coming from the same person who helped her mom cover up a different murder. Thinking wasn't exactly my strong suit lately.

"You still didn't answer my question," my mom spoke over Kurt Cobain's raw vocals.

"What?"

"Did you eat anything while you were out?"

"Oh. Um.., no."

"I can make you something when we get home."

"It's okay, Mom. I'm not really hungry."

"You need to eat something."

"No. What I need is for people to stop worrying about me."

My harsh words escaped before I even realized they were there. I heard my mom exhale through her nose in frustration.

"Emma, I'm trying here. I know things are screwed up, but..,"

"Mom," I interrupted. "I'm sorry. I didn't mean what I said. I've just had a lot on my mind."

"Would you care to talk about it? Maybe it'll help ease your mind."

"Not particularly," I replied. "But.., if the offer still stands, I'll let you make me a grilled cheese sandwich when we get home."

"With tomato?"

"Of course."

"Starting things out on the 90s at 9:00, that was Lithium by Nirvana. Thank you for listening to 103.6, the Pioneer Valley's radio rock hits. I'm your host, Vito Vellone, and for the next hour, I'll be bringing you the best grunge, punk, alternative, and rock the 90s had to offer. But first, in case you're just tuning in, there's some recent breaking news over there in Grancy. Authorities have uncovered a body in the woods outside of the water treatment plant. This station has not received word yet whether they suspect foul play, and no other details have been released at this time. This latest news is coming less than a week after the body of Bellamy High School student Sabrina Beaulieu was found in an abandoned factory. That's some scary happenings for the normally quiet community. Let's send our thoughts and prayers to the folks out there in Grancy, and don't forget to keep it here for all the latest breaking news updates. Now, let's get you back to your favorite 90s hits with Green Day. From

their fifth studio album, Nimrod, this is Good Rid-dance, Time of Your Life."

My eyes widened, and my heart began to race as my stare darted to the radio. In my peripheral vision, I caught my mom biting her nails - something she *never* did. I felt myself gulp as I turned my attention to her.

"Mom, you heard that, right?"

She didn't speak; her gaze remained forward. She slowly nodded while continuing to bite the nail of her index finger. Her eyes were as wide as mine must've been, and her cheeks looked pale in the dim glow of the dash.

I spoke up, my voice raised excitedly. "We've got to do something with the car. If they find out who that body is, it'll lead them right to us. We can't keep it at our house."

"What do we do with it?"

"I don't know," I snapped.

"We can drive it back to Pennsylvania," my mom said in a desperate tone.

"That's a long drive, Mom. If one of us gets pulled over for any reason, we're both screwed."

"Then, what?"

"I don't know yet. I'll think of something. Just give me a day."

"What if we don't have a day?"

"Not helping, Mom. Listen, they don't know who he is. He's not from around here, and they shouldn't be able to identify him. I took care of his fingerprints, and you...," I paused, not wanting to traumatize her more. "Well, his face is unrecognizable. We'll figure it out. I'll come up with something, and then we'll take care of it when I get home from school tomorrow."

My mom shook her head from side to side, mumbling.

"This is wrong; this is all wrong."

"It's not wrong, Mom!" I yelled. "Do you want to go to prison? Because that's what will happen if you tell the police. You invited a man who tried to kill you back into your life, and he ended up dead. That doesn't exactly scream self-defense; it screams revenge."

"We can't keep this up," she argued. "They'll find out."

"They're not going to find out," I retorted, my voice panicky. "We took care of everything. We were careful. We just need to do something with the car. That's all. I'll straighten this out. I just need to think, okay? Let me think. Tomorrow. I'll have something tomorrow."

We both became silent, letting Alanis Morisette's "You Oughta Know" fill the void. It was funny how people's minds worked in times of stress. I should have been hyperventilating, wondering how I'd gotten myself into such a mess. Instead, I was thinking about the song and how thankful I was that "Time of Your Life" wasn't followed by "Ironic." I don't think I could have handled that.

Chapter 30

It Comes Around

The words on the page hadn't changed since the first three times I read them, yet I still had no idea what they said. I couldn't concentrate on English Lit when so many other things wrestled for the top spot on my mind.

Number one on my list of reasons to scream was Travis' car. I needed to come up with something. Mom's idea to drive it back to Pennsylvania was the best option but also the most risky. That was a lot of driving. One misstep – a fender bender, a broken tail light, speeding, failure to come to a complete stop – it was all over. Goodbye freedom, hello orange jumpsuit. I don't look good in orange, so I think I'll pass.

Number two was my growing suspicion of Liza being Sabrina's killer. I wished it wasn't warranted, but she was there that night. She had a knife, and she had a motive. It practically wrote itself. Only - she seemed sincere when she said she didn't kill Sabrina. I wanted to believe her, but she already hid secrets from me. How could I trust her?

As awful as it sounded, I wish Sabrina's boyfriend, Ricky, was the killer. I mean.., if he had found out his girlfriend was cheating on him with another girl, it could have led him to that act of violence. Unfortunately, he had a solid alibi. He was working at the grocery store that night. Detective Harrison confirmed it with the store manager. I don't know; maybe he snuck away unseen, ran the two miles to the abandoned building, killed Sabrina, and then ran back without anyone noticing he was ever gone. Yeah, sure. That made sense. He could explain away the sweat as having overactive glands. Dumb. He didn't do it; that much was clear.

Number three – was someone else there before Liza arrived? That would explain the soda bottle. It could also be who killed Sabrina. That was Patti's bottle, and Patti has yet to explain where she was that night. I already caught her in one lie; could she have others? Was she hiding something sinister behind that innocent, naïve smile of hers? That was almost more unbelievable than Ricky sneaking away from work. Patti was harmless. Wasn't she?

And finally, number four was the mystery texts I kept receiving, including the latest one I had waiting for me on my phone when I woke up this morning. I flipped my phone over on my desk and clicked on the messages to remind myself what it was.

You wait. You'll get yours.

Yeah, I'll get mine. Take a number, whoever you are. My plate's a little full at the moment. Step to the back of the line and wait your turn.

"Hey," Liza whispered, tapping her fingers on my desk to get my attention. I put my phone down and looked over at her. "Didn't you hear me?" she asked.

I shook my head. I had no idea what she was talking about. Was I *that* lost in my thoughts?

"I said, thank you for helping me last night."

I nodded. "Yeah."

"And for believing me," she continued.

That was the gut shot. I put on my "best friend" face and nodded again. "Of course."

"Sshhh!" Mrs. Wendelbaum's voice rang out. "There should be no talking."

I heard a few students snicker while others glanced around curiously to see who was talking. I buried my nose in my textbook to avoid the awkward glares. Liza did the same.

We were all seniors, graduating in less than three weeks. Our class assignment didn't really matter, but Mrs. Wendelbaum had a nasty reputation. The last thing you wanted was to get on her bad side. She could make your last three weeks miserable. Regardless, I still couldn't concentrate on the chapter and found my eyes wandering in Liza's direction. Her dark makeup and goth clothing were a disguise, hiding the sweet, vulnerable girl she was underneath. At least, that's what I thought. Maybe she wasn't sweet at all, and *that* was the disguise.

Just then, a paper airplane hit my hand before coming to a crash landing on my desk. I picked up the plane and peeked back in the direction from which it came. A couple of boys in the back erupted in laughter, alerting the teacher. Mrs. Wendelbaum immediately glanced up and noticed the airplane in my hand.

"I'm glad to see you're making such constructive use of your time, Miss Murphy," she screeched sarcastically.

The entire class peered over at me.

"You weren't planning to throw that airplane in my classroom, were you?"

"No, it wasn't..,"

"Bring it here, please." She tapped her index finger on her desk. "Now!"

More snickers and giggles sounded.

Mrs. Wendelbaum shut that down instantly.

"Hush now! There will be none of that." Her eyes scanned back and forth across the students.

As I made my way to deliver the paper airplane to the designated spot on the teacher's desk, the bell rang, saving me from further humiliation. Students kicked their chairs out as one, racing to be the first out of the classroom. I had to go back to my desk to gather my things, which all but guaranteed my last-place finish in the race.

"I'm very disappointed in you, Miss Murphy. I didn't take you for a troublemaker."

I shook my head at her comment.

"Yeah, well, you never really know someone, do you?"

I walked to the exit and turned back to make one more comment.

"By the way, you really should leave that bottle of vodka at home. Imagine what the faculty would say if someone found it in that hollowed-out book in your bottom drawer. It certainly wouldn't look good for your career."

Mrs. Wendelbaum's jaw dropped, and her eyes widened.

I smiled and walked out. That felt good. Sure, I should be upset; it was another secret lost. But it was for the good of future generations.

Liza waited for me out in the hall. She was shaking her head as I approached.

"I heard what you said in there. Is it true?"

"It is. I was snooping for a hall pass one day and found it."

"One of these days, it's going to come around and bite you."

"Believe me, these days, it feels like teeth are already chewing on me."

"Well, I've gotta get to class. Will I see you after school?"

"I can't," I replied. "I've gotta get home right away."

"Okay, well, thanks again for last night."

"Sure."

Liza walked away, and I looked at the airplane in my hand.

Airplane. That's it! I've got it! Why didn't I think of it before? Mom will be so relieved.

One problem down; on to the next.

Chapter 31

Where The Truth Lies

It was horrible timing on my part. I turned the corner at the wrong moment and witnessed Patti kissing Chris. It was only a little peck on the lips, but something about seeing it still made me say "eww" out loud. Thankfully, I was far enough away they didn't hear me. Even more thankfully, I was close enough to the bathrooms in case the urge to barf came upon me. Chris smiled and lightly tapped the tip of her nose before turning and walking away to his next class. Patti stood and stared at him like a lovesick puppy, squeezing her textbook to her chest in a hug. Oh, brother. She was so lost behind her heart-shaped eyes that she didn't hear me approaching from behind.

"Patti," I called out.

"The one and only," she began enthusiastically, whipping herself around, "but not the.., oh, it's you."

"Yeah, it's me. We need to talk."

I grabbed her forearm and pulled at it, leading her toward the bathroom.

"Can it wait?" she asked. "I'm gonna be late for class."

Funny how you weren't so concerned a moment ago when you were drooling all over Chris, I thought.

"No, it *can't* wait," I replied. "Your teacher will have to somehow manage without you."

I led her into the girl's room and quickly peeked across the bottoms of the stalls to look for any stragglers. No legs. But after remembering how Patti tucked hers up to avoid detection when she was "not spying" on Liza and Sabrina, I thought it best to check each door. When all was clear, I turned toward Patti with conviction and sneered. She jumped skittishly and backed into the wall like she thought I was going to harm her.

"Spill it, Patti," I demanded. "Where were you the night Sabrina was killed?"

"I...I was with Mrs. Donaldson. We were testing the sound system for graduation."

"You can stop lying, Patti. I know that isn't true. The police know it also. You were there at the old mill building that night. Weren't you?"

She shook her head nervously. "No, I...I. I mean.., I wasn't." She stiffened, and her face became white.

"Patti, I know all about it, so you might as well come clean." I was bluffing, of course. I didn't know anything. But she didn't know that.

"But I..,"

"Patti!" I shouted.

She twitched, squeezing her book even tighter.

"Okay, okay; I was there," she admitted.

I felt my insides twist, but I had to keep a strong appearance.

"But it's not what you think," she continued. "I didn't kill Sabrina."

"Then, convince me. Tell me what you were doing there."

"I thought you guys were lying to me about not having the party. I didn't want to be left out. I'm always left out."

She tilted her head to the ground with a sorrowful look and bit the corner of her bottom lip.

"I just wanted to be included, for once, you know? So I went there and hoped you guys wouldn't be too upset with me for crashing the party. But then, there was no party."

"We told you that," I griped.

"I know, and I should have believed you. I'm sorry."

"Whatever. It's fine. So then what?"

"So then I got to thinking how stupid I was for not believing you guys. But I was there, and I hadn't been before, and I thought it would be cool to check the place out. I thought it might give me ideas for one of my fanfic stories."

"So, you were able to get in?"

"Not at first; they had everything locked up pretty good."

"Let me guess.., you were the one who pried open the door on the side of the building."

"Yeah. It was the only one that shook when I tried to open it. Wait.., how did you know about that?"

"Doesn't matter," I replied. "Keep going."

She shot me an inquiring look but didn't argue.

"Well, I went inside and walked around the first floor for a little while, checking out the different rooms; it's *really* cool in there."

Patti's face lit up with excitement.

"It got the wheels in my head turning, and I had to get the ideas down on paper. I pulled my backpack off, sat against the side wall where I'd first gone in, and..,"

"Wait, wait," I halted her. "You brought your backpack to a party?"

"Um, *hello?* There was no party. You already know that."

I closed my eyes tightly in frustration and rubbed my forehead to relieve the tension Patti was causing me. *Why must I deal with imbecilic people*, I thought. I let out a deep breath and opened my eyes, trying so very hard not to scream. With a faked smile, I calmly responded.

"Go on."

"I unzipped my pack to grab my notebook, and my soda bottle fell out and rolled across the floor."

"So it *was* you who brought the bottle!" I said through clenched teeth.

"I'd forgotten I'd had it until then," Patti replied. "I didn't think much of it at the time. Why would I? I was too busy organizing my thoughts into a coherent story on the page. So, I wrote for a little while, but then I had to pee. I remembered seeing a bathroom down one of the side corridors. I knew the plumbing wasn't working, but a toilet's a toilet. I grabbed my book and my pack and went searching for it. I never made it, though. I heard someone's voice call out, and I got freaked. I ran to the nearest window, unlocked it, and got out of there as fast as I could. I ran away, hoping whoever it was didn't spot me. I couldn't get caught sneaking into a building. Not after I.., well, I didn't want to get in trouble."

"So you ran off and have no idea who the other person was?"

"I didn't then, but now I know it must have been Sabrina."

She didn't know. She had no idea Liza was there that night.

"Are you lying to me, Patti? Did you go back and kill Sabrina?"

"What? No!" she exclaimed emphatically. "I would never."

Maybe I was becoming soft, but looking into her terrified eyes, I believed her. Or maybe, like me, she was good at hiding things. Speaking of which..,

"Why are your fingerprints on record?" I asked. She seemed to be in a giving mood, so I thought I'd keep pressing her.

"What?"

"Your fingerprints," I reiterated. "They were on the bottle, like mine, and the police knew to question both of us. That means your fingerprints were in the system. Why?"

"I... I."

She looked fearful, shaking her head from side to side.

"*Tell me*, Patti!" I slapped my palm against the cinderblock wall beside her head. She jumped and immediately spilled it.

"Shoplifting!" she yelled. "I was caught shoplifting."

I was taken aback and stepped a few feet from her.

"You.., shoplifted?" I questioned, trying to hold back a giggle.

She nodded in embarrassment. "A few months before you got here."

"What did you steal?" I questioned.

She hesitated, then came out with it. "A bra."

"A bra?"

"Okay, it was three, but yeah. From Victoria's Secret. My parents never let me wear anything sexy."

That was true, I thought.

"I think that's why I never had any luck with boys."

Oh, you think that's the reason?

"I swore I wasn't going to graduate high school a virgin. I thought if I wore something sexy, it would make me *feel* sexy, and it would somehow, you know, make others see that too. But I didn't know what I was doing and got caught. The store called the police, and I got arrested. I spent an hour in a cell until my parents came to bail me out. They were so disappointed in me. The judge ruled that I'd be placed on probation for a year and had to do community service for a month. Nobody knows about it, Emma; please don't tell anyone."

"I'm not going to tell anyone," I assured her. *Unless you give me a reason to*, I thought.

Just then, my pocket vibrated. I pulled my phone out and must have displayed a nervous look.

"What's wrong?" Patti asked.

"It's nothing," I said.

"It doesn't look like nothing," she continued. "I don't think I've seen you like that before. Who was it?"

"It's nobody, okay?" I barked.

Patti put her head to her chest. "Oh."

How did she do that? How could she make you feel so guilty with a single word? And it wasn't even a word; it was more like a vowel. I swear it was her superpower. Look at me, geeking out like that.

"I'm sorry, Patti. But really, it's nobody. At least, nobody I know. I keep getting texts from this person who's threatening me. Sort of."

"What? Really?"

"Yeah."

"I can help!" she said excitedly. "I mean, *Chris* can. Probably. He works at Radio Hack and knows all about phones and stuff. He could probably find out who the messages are coming from."

"For real?"

"Uh-huh. He's working tonight if you want to go."

Ugh! Always the worst times.

"I can't tonight, Patti, but thanks. I'll keep it in mind. And.., thanks for telling me about that night. It clears up a few things. And don't worry; I won't tell anyone. You're secret's safe with me."

"Thanks, Emma. Is it all right if I go now?"

"Oh, yeah. You can go."

Patti scurried from the girl's room like a rodent just released from its cage, her head hung low, her chin resting on the books she still clenched tightly to her chest. I couldn't help but feel sorry for her. She was such a sad, nerdy girl. Or was it all an act? I still didn't know for sure. Her naïve behavior seemed genuine, but I've been off my mark lately. I wasn't sure I could trust my own judgment. At least she was willing to volunteer her boyfriend's services to help with my unwanted secret admirer. Maybe I'd soon have another problem solved. I glanced at my phone again and sighed.

I should kill you for what you did to me.

Chapter 32

One More Down

“The airport!” I yelled, barging into the house. “I figured it out!”

My mom came barreling around the corner. “What are you screaming about?” she asked.

“The car,” I answered. “We can park it at the airport. They have long-term parking services. I looked it up; it can be there for up to a month if we need it to be.”

“I don’t know, honey,” my mom responded, rubbing her index finger across her lower lip. “That can get awfully expensive.”

“Mom!” I threw my palms facing up in front of me like two holders on a scale. “Expensive,” I said, shaking one hand, “or prison?” I shook the other more emphatically to make my point. "Now, let's go. It's perfect."

She hesitated, her eyes shifting back and forth as if trying to think of another option. There wasn't one. Short of finding an illegal chop shop that would strip the car clean, this was the best we had.

"Okay," she nodded.

"Good, now let's go. The sooner the car is away from here, the better."

"Let me grab my things," my mom insisted.

I patiently waited in the foyer for her return, if continually tapping my foot on the floor was a sign of patience. While I had nothing better to do than be annoyed at how long my mom was taking, I thought about my conversations with Liza and Patti. I couldn't believe they were both at the crime scene the night of Sabrina's murder. Patti was the first there. That much was established by Liza when she recalled seeing the soda bottle already in the building when she arrived. Patti claimed she took off when she heard a voice call out. That was Liza. But what if Patti didn't leave like she said she had? What if she ducked into that bathroom she mentioned? It wouldn't be the first time she hid away, listening to Liza and Sabrina's conversation. Then, after Liza left, she came out of the bathroom and..,

What? She stabbed Sabrina with her toy lightsaber or Harry Potter wand? Get real, Emma.

Liza, on the other hand, admitted to having a knife. If Patti left as she said she had, then Liza was the only other person with Sabrina. She asked Sabrina to meet her there; she brought a knife, and Sabrina ended up dead. Then, Liza carelessly lost the murder weapon and asked for my help to find it, no doubt to get rid of the evidence. The pieces couldn't fit any better. Unless.., there was someone else there. Did one of the cheerleaders go back? But why? Why would any of them want to hurt their teammate? Jealousy? Revenge? I dug deep into my well of secrets to try and pull something from it, but I kept coming up empty. I had nothing.

I pulled out my phone to text Liza, but my thumb hovered motionless over the screen. What was I going to say? Outright accuse her of killing Sabrina? She was my best friend. And I had no proof. I couldn't do it. I wouldn't do it. I didn't want to do it.

"Okay, I'm ready." My mom startled me.

Thank God for small favors. If another few seconds went by, I might have started typing. It might not have been nice.

"My mom pulled out her keys and handed me the set to the Camaro (I trained her well). As weird as it was, I got a little giddy about that. The car was older than I was, so I shouldn't have felt that way, but Detective Harrison said it best: it was a pretty sweet ride.

"I'll follow you," I began, "but when we get there, you go to the departure drop-off area, and I'll meet you there after I park the car."

"Please, be careful, Emma."

"I'm always careful," I replied.

My mom's expression became grim - like she disagreed.

"I *am*, Mom," I repeated with conviction.

She huffed, slightly shook her head, and opened the door.

"Oh, wait," I said, running toward the kitchen.

I opened up the junk drawer in the cabinet by the fridge and rummaged through it until I found what I was looking for, then ran back to the front door.

"Okay, now we can go."

The Airport was about forty-five minutes away, a little over the state line into Connecticut. I requested to take the back roads so we wouldn't have to deal with highway traffic. The state police were always pulling vehicles over for one reason or another. I didn't want to take the chance. Who cared if it took a little longer - as long as we got there without incident?

It was a calm ride, which allowed my frantic thoughts to settle. I turned on the radio for some background noise, not anticipating I'd cause myself more stress. The radio had other ideas.

"...not what I'm saying, Vito. The police need to do a better job of protecting our citizens. First, a high school student, and now a body is found in the

woods. We're not some big city where crime is running rampant, and yet, we've seen two murders in a week with no suspects."

"Well, I think you just made my point, Cheryl. Crime isn't running rampant in Grancy. I think that's in large part due to the police force. I'm not saying the system is perfect, but we should be supporting the men and women in law enforcement. Especially since the crime rate is so low."

"Supporting, yes, but still holding them accountable for doing their jobs."

"But what aren't they doing, Cheryl? They're in the middle of an investigation. They're not sitting on their hands, hoping a killer will step forward."

"Do you know that for sure, Vito? I haven't seen them doing much in the community to make people feel safe."

"Well, I don't make a habit of stepping into our schools to watch over our teachers either, Cheryl, but I put my faith in them that they are doing the best job they can to educate our children."

"But, at least we get updates from our children."

"I suppose some parents do if they're lucky. I'm also confident the police are telling us what they can when they can. Folks - in case you're just tuning in, my guest in the studio this evening is Cheryl Lombardi of the Teacher's Advocacy Committee. Now, Cheryl, I have to ask. Why has *the latest news about the John Doe body found in Grancy caused such a stir with your group?"*

"Because, Vito, it's every teacher's responsibility to look after the students. The police haven't shared anything with the public other than to say the victim found outside the water treatment plant was believed to be murdered. How do we know that crime isn't somehow connected to Sabrina Beaulieu's murder? Our kids are afraid to leave their homes. They aren't concentrating in school, and they feel very unsafe. And that was only after the first murder. Sabrina's classmates, friends, teammates.., it's hit everyone hard, including the educators and faculty. Now that there is a second suspected homicide, the students and staff are even more shaken. How do we convince them that they're safe if the police won't share what they know and reassure the community there isn't a deranged killer on the loose?"

"I think you're blowing this out of proportion. It's a little early to expect..."

I clicked off the radio as I turned right into the long-term parking lot. My mom continued straight, heading toward the departure area. What did I get from that laughable interview? Well, if the police knew anything about the victim's identity, they would have shared that by now. The fact that they listed him as a John Doe means they're still in the dark. I hope. That's a huge relief.

I pulled the ticket from the kiosk and watched the gate lift to allow me entrance. I drove around a bit, looking for a spot in the center. Once parked, I read the back of the ticket. It said to remove any personal and/or valuable items from the vehicle. Easy enough. I swept my eyes across the back seat. There was nothing there of any value. I leaned over and opened the glove compartment. If the car got broken into, I didn't want the registration to be our downfall. I pulled out the few loose sheets of paper and sifted through them. There was an inspection report, a registration document, and..,

Okay, that's strange. Travis kept the title to the vehicle in his glove compartment. Who does that? That confirmed it for me - Travis was an idiot. Sadly, that kind of made my mom an even bigger idiot for liking him in the first place.

I folded up the papers and tucked them into my back pocket, swapping them with what I grabbed from the junk drawer: a screwdriver. I ran across the parking lot to the farthest car from the entrance and removed its plates. *Sorry, whoever you are*, I thought. *I need them more than you.*

People didn't really pay attention to whether or not they had plates, did they? There was always the chance I'd return them before the owner showed up to get their car. Maybe.

I ran back to the Camaro and took off the plates, replacing them with the ones I "borrowed." After that, I locked the doors, tucked the plates under my arm, and casually walked out of the parking lot to meet my mom.

I was feeling pretty good. Confident. Everything was going to work out. We weren't completely out of the woods yet, but at least, for a little while, we were in the clear.

Chapter 33

Burned

Daydreaming during homeroom while Mr. Dodd took attendance wasn't always my thing. I was the girl who was always laser-focused. Lately, however, my thoughts had been scattered and disjointed. Could you blame me? Between my mom killing her ex-boyfriend and me helping to cover it up, the authorities finding the body, and the gnawing feeling in my gut that one of my closest friends might have killed a classmate, I wasn't exactly living your typical teenage life. I was graduating in less than three weeks, and my life was a mess. My mom was on the verge of having a nervous breakdown, some rando psycho was sending me threatening text messages, and my best friend..,

My head remained forward as my eyes shifted sideways to notice Liza writing something on a piece of paper she'd torn from her notebook. It wasn't so much her sudden desire to write instead of chat with me that piqued my curiosity. It was how she was using her left hand to shield her words. That hardly seemed fair. How was I supposed to learn things when she was being so secretive? How was I supposed to trust her? She used to share everything with me, but now, it was like she was a different person. I wasn't sure how much I liked this new Liza. But I knew how much I was beginning to dislike her.

The bell sounded, causing my slouched body to flinch and sit upright in my chair. Liza swiped the paper from her desk and crumpled it into a ball. I guess she wasn't satisfied with her writing. I stood up, watching her gather her notebook into her pack, waiting for her to acknowledge me. I was too impatient.

"I'm going to Radio Hack after school today if you want to join me," I said.

"What's at Radio Hack?" Liza asked, finally recognizing she wasn't alone in this world.

"Believe it or not," I answered, "Chris Green. He works there. I've been having some issues with my phone recently, and Patti suggested I have him check it out."

"Oh, Patti suggested that, huh?"

"Yeah."

"I guess you guys are like best friends now."

"What? Where did that come from?"

"You don't think I notice you two hanging out in the halls, whispering to each other? Give me a break. I know what you're doing; it's so blatant."

"What are you talking about?" I asked, agitated.

She got up from her desk and slung her backpack over her shoulder.

"You've probably been telling her..," she paused, looked around the room to see who was still present, then quieted her voice to a whisper, "...about the knife."

"What?" I questioned, flabbergasted she would think that of me. "I wouldn't do that," I said in a hushed voice. "I promised you."

"Yeah, well, you also promised me you wouldn't tell people about me and Sabrina. You were the only one who knew about us, and now it's out there."

"Wait – I didn't..,"

Liza stormed away before I could get the words out. I watched her toss the crumpled paper into the trash can as she walked by Mr. Dodd's desk. What was she talking about, anyway? I didn't tell anybody about her relationship with Sabrina. But also, I wasn't the only person who knew about it.

Patti, what did you do?

Shit! Add another thing to my already complicated life. Now I had to find out why Patti would blab about that. I only hoped Liza would believe me when I told her I had nothing to do with it.

I composed myself and walked toward the door, hoping I could catch Liza at her locker before things worsened between us. Something stopped me from exiting. I turned my head and looked over my shoulder. Mr. Dodd was sitting at his desk, filling out paperwork, unaware he still had a student in his classroom. Beside his desk was the trash can.

I shouldn't, I thought. *She already thinks I betrayed her trust. Then again, since she already thinks it, what would be the harm? You're right, Emma. I should.*

I walked back toward Mr. Dodd's desk, hoping not to disturb him; no such luck.

"Is there something you need, Emma?" he asked, looking up from his subject pad.

"Oh, no, Mr. Dodd. I accidentally dropped something out of my bag," I said convincingly. I pointed to the floor by his basket. "Oh, here it is."

"Well, I'm glad you didn't lose it," he responded, turning his nose back to his paperwork.

I bent over, retrieved the balled-up note from the bin, and tossed it into my bag's front pocket. As I headed back to leave, I heard a commotion out in the hall and a loud banging noise, like someone punched a locker. I hustled out to find a small crowd gathered near the water fountains. In the middle of that crowd, backed against a row of lockers, was Liza, her cheek showing a streak of black where a tear had escaped. In front of her, with hatred in his eyes, was Ricky, Sabrina's boyfriend. The other students were egging him on like a bunch of torchbearers on their way to lighting up their first witch at the stake.

"It was you, wasn't it, you bitch!" Ricky seethed. "You were jealous she was with me."

Liza reached up and rubbed the back of her head while wincing and shaking it in denial. That explained the loud banging noise. Liza didn't like me right now, and I wasn't sure how I felt about her, but there was no way I was letting this happen. I rushed into the crowd, squeezing myself through.

"*You* killed her, didn't you?" Ricky continued, lumbering forward. "You couldn't stand that she wasn't into girls. She wasn't a lesbian like you, freak."

"Kick her ass," someone yelled from the crowd.

Just what the situation needed – some idiotic dumbass getting the crowd going. Ricky stepped forward threateningly and shoved Liza's shoulder back.

"Don't touch her!" I shouted, breaking through the line into the center. Liza glared over at me with a look that was a cross between confusion and anger.

"Oh look," Ricky began, "your little girlfriend has come to defend your honor."

"Shut the hell up, Ricky," I said, my teeth clasped shut.

"Or what, Emma? What are you going to do about it?"

I looked around at the smirking faces, the mob eager for violence and blood. I looked back at Ricky, my mind shuffling through pages and pages of secrets, seeking what I needed to end this hostility before it got further out of hand. That was when I realized.., I had nothing. Ricky was clean. There wasn't a speck of dirt I could drum up about him. Like Liza, he was just an innocent victim of Sabrina's cruel game. *Was Liza innocent, though?* Was Ricky really angry or just embarrassed that Sabrina might not have loved him as much as he thought? I hated being in the middle of this drama, especially without ammo.

"I'm not going to do anything, jackhole," I responded.

"What did you call me?"

"What's the matter, can't handle the truth? It takes a real, big man to shove a girl around. Your parents must be proud. I can hear them now, *'That's our boy, the woman beater.'*"

"Shut up!" he yelled.

"Why? One girl's not enough? You're going to beat on two?"

"I said shut up!"

Ricky stepped forward, his fist clenched. I didn't expect that; I thought I could get him to back down. Instead, I recognized the same look displayed on his face as Travis had just before he clocked my mom in the face. I knew what was coming. I closed my eyes and braced myself.

"Mr. Meyers!" the voice of salvation called out. "What do you think you're doing?"

I never cared for Mr. Dodd as much as I did at that moment. The gathered students scattered in all directions like cockroaches.

"I wasn't doing nothin'," Ricky replied.

Way to go, brainiac, I thought, *admitting your guilt by using a double negative.*

"I see," responded Mr. Dodd. "Then you won't mind explaining your case to the principal."

"But I..,"

"Ah, ah," Mr. Dodd interrupted, wagging his finger. "Principal Malik's office. Now!"

Ricky's tense shoulders dropped. He glanced at Liza, whose face showed uncomfortable concern. *Was it for me?* Ricky then turned his stare toward me. Luckily, Mr. Dodd was standing behind me, so he couldn't see the arrogant grin I had plastered on my face. Ricky's eyes narrowed in contempt. Fortunately, there was nothing he could do but tuck his tail between his legs and drag his feet on his way to the principal's office. I wanted to scream, "Have a good chat with Principal Malik," but that would have been a bit much, even for me.

"Are you girls okay?" Mr. Dodd queried.

We answered in unison.

"Yeah."

"Yes, Mr. Dodd."

"Good, then I expect you to get to your class-rooms. Move along now."

He waved the back of his hand forward to hurry us along. We quietly turned and walked down the hall. I saw Liza glance over her shoulder to check the status of our homeroom teacher. He hadn't budged from his position. We took a hard right at the end of the hallway, and once out of sight of the older teacher, Liza yanked my shoulder, forcing me to turn toward her.

"I didn't need your help back there," she fumed.

"You could've fooled me," I replied.

"Well, I didn't. It's your fault I was in that mess anyway. You *had* to open your big mouth, didn't you?"

"Liza, I didn't tell anybody."

"Yeah, right. If not you, then who?"

That was an easy one, but what was I to do? I just saved one friend from a lynching. Could I sacrifice another at the altar? I didn't betray Liza's trust, and I couldn't betray Patti's either.

"I...I don't know."

"How convenient," Liza responded snidely. "I thought you were my friend, but you're just like all the rest. I can't believe I trusted you."

My heart sank. Liza walked away.

Come back, my thoughts roared, but my lips said nothing. Why would they? Even they were smart enough to know I'd just lost my best friend.

Chapter 34

Out

The minute hand clicked so slowly. No matter what the experts said, I thought watching paint dry might have actually been faster than whatever that clock was doing. It didn't help that my head was not in a good space. Liza was no longer my friend and was avoiding me like the plague. Patti managed to elude me all day and had somehow ducked into her last-period classroom before I could get my mitts on her. I never thought I'd be annoyed being ignored by Patti. I should be celebrating. If only I thought it would help. Why didn't I tell Liza it was Patti who ratted her out? The easy answer was that I wasn't positive it *was* Patti. Yeah, right. It had to be. The true answer was a purely selfish one. I still needed Patti, or rather, Patti's boyfriend, to solve my text message problem. Another one came in earlier today. It read:

If I ever run into you alone somewhere,
you're dead. You hear me? DEAD!

That was a fun one. Like I wasn't already an emotional wreck before that came in. Thanks a lot, anonymous scumbag. It's so easy for you to threaten me through a screen. Maybe you should hope we *don't* meet up. If we did, I'd.., I'd..,

Argh! I couldn't even think of anything. I just wanted to get the hell out of there. My eyes drifted to the clock again. Really? It hadn't even been two minutes since I checked it last. Someone get me a paintbrush.

Twenty-four grueling minutes later, the final bell rang. Misty Ludwitz, who sat in front of me, should be grateful. I was on the cusp of stabbing her in the neck with my pencil to entertain myself. *Sorry, Sabrina*, I thought.

Whatever. It was over. I could now search out Patti. Maybe I'd bump into Liza on my way, and we could hash things out. Was that too much to ask?

Apparently, it was - since there was no sign of Liza anywhere. Did she leave early again? It didn't matter; Patti was in my sight. I had a bone to pick.

I hurried over to her before she could disappear again.

"Patti!" I called out.

"The one and only. But not the one and..,"

"Will you shut up already?" I'd heard enough. She clammed up tighter than a.., well, a clam. "I need you to meet me out back," I demanded.

"But I was going to say goodbye to Chris before I left."

"You can call him later," I replied. "This is important."

I played on Patti's neediness. That I had something important to say, and I was including her, only made her want to meet me that much more. I quickly walked away but could hear her footsteps following behind. That was too easy. Maybe I still had the magic after all.

I popped out the rear entrance and leaned against the brick exterior, waiting for Patti to join me. When she finally exited, I pushed my shoulder from the wall and crossed my arms about my chest, the dour expression on my face smashed headlong into her cheery mug. Her smile quickly faded.

"What's wrong, Emma?" she asked.

"How could you tell everyone about Liza and Sabrina?"

I saw Patti's throat tighten as she gulped.

"Ah ha!" I said in a raised voice, pointing my finger at her. "It *was* you."

"No, you don't understand," Patti said. "It wasn't me. But it *is* my fault."

"What does that mean?" I questioned.

"My parents and I got called into the police station last night. That detective guy..,"

"Detective Harrison," I interjected.

"Yeah, him. He had more questions for me."

"I warned you, Patti. I told you the police knew you lied about being with Mrs. Donaldson that night."

"I know. And with my parents there, I couldn't bring myself to lie anymore."

"So, what..? You..,"

"I told them!" she blurted. "I told them I was at the old mill building that night."

Holy shit! I wasn't expecting that. I *did* still have the magic.

"I explained everything to them: the soda bottle, my overactive bladder, how someone else showed up, and I took off for fear I'd get caught."

"And they believed you?"

She feigned dumb. "Why wouldn't they? It's true."

Wait, this was Patti. She might actually *be* dumb.

"Okay, hold on." I stopped her and began rubbing my temples. "I'm getting lost here. What does that have to do with you telling everyone about Sabrina and Liza's relationship?"

"I told you, I didn't."

Patti began biting her lower lip.

"I feel a 'but' coming on," I said.

"I sorta told the detective."

"You 'sorta' told the..,"

I stopped to take a deep breath.

"Why would you do that? You knew how that would make Liza look."

"He kept asking me if I wanted to share anything else. I said 'no,' but he kept asking as if he knew I was holding onto something. I didn't want to say anything. He kept pressuring me."

"So you told him they were seeing each other?"

She hesitated, then nodded, dropping her eyes to the ground out of guilt.

"But I didn't tell him about the argument," Patti stated enthusiastically.

"Big whoop," I commented. "They're still going to see her as a suspect now."

"Well, I mean, she could be," Patti squeaked out softly.

"How can you still believe that?"

"I'm trying to think of Sabrina," Patti said. "I can't keep worrying about hurting someone's feelings. Sabrina is dead; somebody killed her. Wouldn't you want her killer facing justice – even if it was your best friend?"

Patti's words hit me like a freight train. For all her absurdities and naivety, she was right. It was about justice for Sabrina. I couldn't keep protecting Liza, no matter how close we were. I couldn't condemn her either if I didn't think she did it. And I didn't.

"So you told the police about Liza and Sabrina," I continued in a calmer voice. "But how did everyone at school learn about it?"

"It had to be Jill," Patti answered.

"Jill? How would she have known?"

"She was at the police station too. When we were finally free to go, Jill was sitting with her parents in the hall, waiting to talk with Detective Harrison. My mother stopped and asked if they'd gotten called in as well. They did."

"After learning about it from you," I added, "Detective Harrison must have asked Jill if she knew anything about Liza and Sabrina. So.., Jill told everyone in school. That bitch!"

Patti shrugged her shoulders. "I don't know. Maybe."

"Wait until I get my hands on her," I said, clenching my fists.

"You're not going to hurt her, are you?"

I wanted to. I'd do it now if Jill were here.

"No," I said. "But I'm sure going to have it out with her."

"Phew."

I rubbed my forehead to keep the imminent pounding at bay.

"Is that all, Emma?"

"Yeah," I said quickly without thought. "Wait, no. Can I still have Chris look at my phone?"

Patti smiled. "Of course. He was going to work right after school. If you want to go there now, we can walk together."

Ugh! Why did I ask? Shoot me now.

"Sure, Patti," I nodded. "Why not?"

Chapter 35

Whose Line is it Anyway

We made it to Radio Hack – both alive. Though, I don't mind telling you, there were times I wanted to strangle Patti to get her to shut up. Obviously, I didn't do that because I'm a nice girl. Plus, there are already way too many dead people around me.

I was the first through the door. Chris was behind the counter, playing with a spool of register tape. How exciting. He looked up at me and nodded. Did I expect him to jump over the counter and greet me with open arms? No. But would it have killed him to smile? Then Patti walked in, and everything changed. Chris' face lit up like a Christmas tree.

"Patti, you're here!" he said with an elevated excitement in his voice.

"Hi, Poopsie Bear," Patti responded.

Give me a break. That wasn't what I signed up for when I agreed to come here. If that kind of talk continued, I'd lose my lunch.

"What are you doing here, babe?"

"Well, since I missed you after school today," Patti replied, "I thought I'd surprise you with my presence."

"I'm happy you did," Chris said.

Patti leaned over the counter, and Chris moved forward, their lips meeting in the middle. I cleared my throat to announce I was *also* in the store, in case anyone cared. Also, before I said something about how sick they were making me.

"Oh right," Patti said, turning her attention to me. "Chris, you know my best friend, Emma."

"Just *friend*," I emphasized.

"That's what I said," Patti responded. "Best friend."

I shook my head and pinched the bridge of my nose between my fingers. I knew the probability of getting struck by lightning was some astronomical number - especially indoors - on a sunny day, but if there was ever a chance it could happen to someone, let it be me.

"We know each other," Chris acknowledged. "We're in history together."

"Right," I nodded.

"So you're Patti's friend, huh?"

"*Best* friend," Patti immediately chimed in.

I changed my mind. If lightning were to strike, let it take Patti first.

I let her annoying comment slide off my shoulder. Instead, I smiled that awkward kind of smile you make when a photographer asks you to repeat some ridiculous word to get you to smile, but all you can think about is how uncomfortable you are in the size-too-small shoes you wore because they went so well with the dress that was *two* sizes too small.

"So, what brings you here?"

I pulled my phone from my back pocket and placed it on the counter.

"Patti said you might be able to help me with some strange messages I've been receiving."

"Strange messages?"

"Text messages. I keep getting them, but I don't know who they're from."

"Have you tried blocking them?" Chris asked. "Or even calling them to tell them they have the wrong number?"

"The texts don't come in with any number associated with them, so I can't call or block them. I'm able to text back, though."

"No number associated with them? That's strange. May I?" he asked, pointing to my phone.

I nodded.

Chris picked up my phone and plugged a small, handheld device into it.

"I want to find out who they're coming from," I said.

"That should be no problem," he replied. "Well, most likely. Not everything comes from a registered account, but I can get you close if that's the case."

"Do you need my passcode?"

He shook his head. "Nah. I'm already in." He flashed me the handheld device that displayed my screen on it.

Patti clapped a few times while jumping in place. "This is exciting, isn't it?"

"Sure," I murmured with much less enthusiasm.

"Wow, these are *some* text messages," Chris stated, his eyes bulging.

"Tell me about it," I replied. "Can you figure out who they're from?"

"Hold on a second," he said. He put the phone down and ran off to the back room.

"Didn't I tell you he was great?" Patti said, smiling from ear to ear.

"He hasn't done anything yet," I responded.

Chris came marching back with a little black thumb drive in his hand. He picked up the device connected to my phone and plugged the drive into the side of it.

"What's going on?" I asked. "What are you doing?"

"The messages are being sent using some encryption software. You must have clicked on a bad link at some point, allowing this person to access your device. This little baby," he tapped the thumb drive, "will let me scan for the software device's IP address. Then we can clone the network line, which should give us a number."

"Wait. Clone, as in copy the other person's phone?"

"Not exactly. However, with the right software, you could bounce texts from one phone to another or make it look like texts were coming from someone else."

"You can do that?"

"Sure. There's some crazy malware shit out there. Hustle GP. Scam-i-Cide. CyClone. Warp Bot. It's scary."

"And anyone can get this stuff?"

"Right off the Dark Web. That's how hackers create those phishing scam links. Or you can download it onto an external drive and then install it to whatever device you want to 'infect.' The owner doesn't even know their device has it installed. These days, they're virtually undetectable."

"Wow."

"Yeah. Okay, here we go. I've got a location. The signal is being bounced between cell towers somewhere in Pennsylvania."

"Pennsylvania?" I questioned.

"Hey, isn't that where you're from?" Patti inquired.

"Yeah. Are we lucky enough to get a number?"

"I'm getting there," Chris replied. "I just have to clone the line and.., there."

He flashed the screen to me. 545-361-7729.

"That's the number?" I asked.

"That's the number," he responded. "Need me to write it down for you? Once I unplug it, it goes away."

"I got it, thanks."

"No problem." He unplugged his device and handed my phone back to me. I quickly typed the number into my phone while it was still fresh in my mind. "Anything else I can help you with?"

Can you take your girlfriend out back and put her out of my misery so I don't have to walk home with her?

"No. Thanks, Chris. You've done more than enough."

"Anything for a friend of Patti's."

"*Best* friend," Patti insisted again.

I ignored that comment.

"I should probably get home," I said.

"Um..," Patti began, nibbling the tip of her index finger. "Would you mind walking alone, Emma? I think I'm going to stay here a little longer."

Oh, thank God! Maybe she'll get laid in the back room.

"It's fine, Patti," I answered, trying to hold back my excitement. "I'll manage."

"Okay."

I walked out with a renewed sense of purpose. I had a number. I could work with that. As long as it belonged to someone's real phone and not some burner phone, I could find the asshole who's been sending me those texts. It was all falling into place.

Chapter 36

Crumbs

I had a few hours after dinner to research the phone number Chris pulled from my mysterious messenger. I tried calling it to give the owner a verbal smackdown, but when it connected, there were only a bunch of beeps and clicking sounds. I should have known it wouldn't be that easy.

When I typed the number into my browser's search field, a name immediately popped up on the screen - Carla Wittell. I stared at the name, scratching my head, trying to figure out if I knew that person. Who the hell was Carla Wittell? I didn't know anybody by that name. My tongue slid back and forth along the inside of my lower lip while I painfully tried to recall interactions with

230

people from my previous life. Carla Wittell. Carla Wittell. Nope. I had nothing.

Never one to let that stop me, I pulled up another search screen and typed in the woman's name. There were a handful of hits. Two women were from the 1800s, so they were out. One woman was born in 1936. She was still alive, but she'd be eighty-eight years old. I doubt she even knew how to text, let alone figure out encryption software. There was a thirty-seven-year-old in Australia – not even remotely close to Pennsylvania. And finally, a woman serving a life sentence in a Texas prison. None of them fit the bill.

I ran a few more searches and came up frustratingly empty. Who was that woman, and why was she targeting me? What did she think I did?

I closed my eyes and rubbed my forehead to calm myself. It was getting late, and I was getting nowhere. I decided to call it a night. I grabbed the top of my laptop screen but then froze. I don't know what stopped me from closing it. Something Chris had said sprang into my brain, and I curiously stared at the screen. I brought my fingers to the keyboard and typed: D-A-R-K-W-E-B.

Okay, I thought as I exhaled nervously, *that wasn't so bad.* Turns out, you can't access it without having specific software on your machine. That was probably a good thing. Still, it might have been exciting to see what I could find. Maybe.., maybe there was still a chance. But it'd have to wait until tomorrow. I was exhausted.

Chapter 37

Wind of Change

The Camaro came to a screeching stop inches away from the sidewalk at the front of the school. The sign at the front of my car said "One-hour parking," but that didn't apply to me. I pulled my shades up onto my head and stared out the passenger-side window at the jealous faces gawking at my ride. I heard the first bell ring even with the windows closed and watched the students rush into the front door to get to their classes. I wasn't as concerned. The teachers liked me; they'd wait. I gathered my bag from the front passenger seat and stepped out of the car, admiring myself in the reflection of my driver-side window. Some people had to work hard to look this good. To me, it came naturally.

I kissed my first two fingers and touched them to my lips in the window's reflection. I threw my backpack over my shoulder and casually strolled to the front entrance, my skin-tight, black leather pants hugging my legs, displaying every sexy contour. To the right of the front door, Detective Harrison was helping the landscapers weed the flower bed. He wore a white tank top that displayed his perfectly tanned arms with muscles that glistened with sweat. He saw me approaching and smiled; I knew what he wanted, his eyes trained on my every step. I teased him by flashing a provocative smile of my own, coupled with a wink. That's all he'd get from me.., for now.

I entered the school and immediately noticed the lights were so dim I could barely see the end of the empty hallway. I made my way down the corridor, looking into each classroom, the empty desks within each dark room sending chills down my spine.

"Hello?" I called out. There was no response.

As I neared the last door at the end of the hall, a bright light illuminated through the door's window, creating a distorted rectangle on the floor in front of it.

"Hello?" I called again. "Is somebody in there?"

The door squeaked open, and the light temporarily blinded me. I put my hands up in front of my face to shield my eyes as I stepped through the doorway into the classroom. The door slammed shut behind me, startling me.

The light flickered and returned to a more manageable brightness. A handful of students were gathered before me, standing in a semi-circle. They wore nametags on their chests as if I didn't already know who they were. They waved me forward in silence, their circle slowly opening to reveal an unconscious woman on the floor behind them. My legs became wobbly, and the air chilled to where I could see my breath with every labored exhale, yet my feet trudged forward at my classmates' silent command. Liza was the closest to the woman, and as I approached, she handed me a knife. It had a black handle with a gold-colored ring around it. She pointed to the woman. I nodded and stepped forward, straddling the woman's body. She was an attractive woman with short, curly blonde hair that extended just below her ears. She wore a vibrant red dress with red high heels and long red gloves up to her elbows. I kneeled over her, my legs on either side of her waist. I spotted the nametag clipped to her dress and stared at it, wondering where I'd seen that name before. Carla Wittell. I looked back at the students, and in unison, they extended their arms and pointed at the woman.

"What do you want me to do?" I asked. "I don't know what you want me to do."

Liza opened her mouth and spoke.

"Beep."

I shook my head in confusion.

"What? I don't get it."

Then, in response, all the students opened their mouths and belted out.

"Beep, beep, beep, beep."

The noise was deafening. I covered my ears to escape the sound, but it was useless.

"Beep, beep, beep, beep, beep."

My eyes flew open, and I jumped to a seated position on my bed, my phone's alarm doing a hell of a job waking the dead. I reached over and hit the sleep button.

"What the hell was that?" I mumbled. I didn't usually have such vivid dreams, so it came as a shock how real it all felt. I hoped that wasn't going to be a regular occurrence. My waking life was stressful enough, I didn't need that crap invading my sleep, as well.

I rubbed my face, feeling sorry for myself. I glanced up at the calendar on my wall, the date May 28th circled in thick red ink. *Two weeks*, I thought. *You can do this.* I pushed myself up and dragged my heavy feet to the bathroom. *Damn, I looked good in those pants, though.*

It was painfully clear Liza was either avoiding me by skipping homeroom, or she had stayed home from school. She used to let me know in advance so we could plan a day off together. What was with her? I couldn't believe how quickly she'd changed. She was being a little bitc.., well, she wasn't the same friend I'd gotten to know these past six months. So, she didn't want to be my friend anymore. Fine. We probably wouldn't have seen each other after high school anyway. It was better this way. Wasn't it?

Mr. Dodd finished his attendance just in time for the bell to ring. I headed into the hall and spotted Jill by her locker. Alone. That was unusual, as she always had her cheerleader entourage with her. I stormed over to her, ready to start a fight.

"Hey!" I yelled to her back. "I know what you did, you skanky bitch."

She turned to face me, a trail of unwiped tears still prominent on her cheeks.

"What do you want?" Jill responded, her teeth chattering behind her scowl.

"I...I..." I lost my train of thought. What was happening here? Was I still dreaming? "What's wrong with *you*? Why the tears?"

"They all hate me," she replied. "All of them. I can't believe they turned on me like that. All I did was tell them the truth – that Sabrina was a lesbo and lied to us the whole time."

"She was bi," I said.

"Whatever," Jill hissed. "She still betrayed her friends and her teammates, pretending she was something she wasn't. She made fools of all of us. To think, I let her put lotion on me at the beach. That's not right. At least everyone knew which side of the fence Liza was on. Sabrina was living a lie, and we all fell for her charade."

I shook my head in disgust.

"You skinny little homophobic twat. I almost felt sorry for you. *You're* what's wrong with this messed-up world. Why the hell does it matter who somebody loves? We're all just trying to get by in this shitty life. We don't need people like you bringing the rest of us down. Karma's a real bitch, isn't she? You're getting *exactly* what you deserve."

I walked away, feeling Jill's stare burning into my back. I didn't care. For the first time in a while, I felt good about myself.

Chapter 38

The Webs We Weave

No matter how many times my finger traced along the name I'd written on the paper, it wasn't ringing a bell. I didn't know why it bothered me so much, but it did. Why was it so important for me to learn who Carla was? If Chris was right, and she was in Pennsylvania, then I had nothing to worry about. Her messages were just empty threats. I could ignore the occasional texts that came in. See how easy that was? Problem solved.

My leg bounced up and down as I peered over Chris' shoulder at Mr. Wurth explaining the events of 9/11. I looked back down at Carla's name scribbled in blue ink and felt my shoulders tense. I tried to ignore it; I really did.

Darn it!

238

I reached forward and tapped Chris on the shoulder. He turned his head sideways to see me peripherally.

"I need to access the Dark Web," I whispered.

That got his attention. He sat up and swiveled in his chair to look at me head-on.

"What?"

"I need to access the Dark Web. Can you help me?"

"That's not a good idea," he said softly.

Ignoring his words, I continued.

"I read that you needed special software to access it."

"That's true."

"Can you get it for me?"

"Why do you want to get on there?" he asked.

"I want to find the woman who's been texting me."

"It's a woman?"

"Yeah, but I can't find her in any search on the internet. I bet I'll find her on the Dark Web."

"I don't know..,"

"Can you help me or not?" I asked again, my whisper elevated enough for the history nerds closest to us to take notice. I gave them all dirty looks and pointed forward. They complied.

Chris shook his head as if wrestling with what to do, then reached into his backpack and pulled out a thumb drive. He offered it to me, but when I went to grab it from him, he pulled it back. I saw the nervousness in his eyes.

"I swear," I said, "I won't do anything bad with it. I'm not some crazy person, you know. I only want to find out who the woman is."

Chris sighed silently and handed me the drive.

"Thank you," I said.

"That'll give you access without you having to install anything on your computer. Just plug it in and click on your USB drive. After it loads, go to your browser."

"Awesome! Thank you so much. I'll give it back to you tomorrow."

He nodded and turned back to the front.

Ha, Carla Wittell, I thought. *I've got you now.*

On the walk home, I was getting excited. I twirled the thumb drive in my fingertips, wondering if the *real* Carla looked anything like the woman I pictured in my dream. I hoped not. I wanted her to be ugly. It was easier to hate ugly people. Either way, I'd feel more comfortable when I knew for sure where that woman lived. Unless she lived down the street - then I'd feel less comfortable.

I wonder how Liza's doing?

Where'd that come from? I hated when spontaneous thoughts popped into my head, disturbing the other spontaneous thoughts I was already thinking. *Did* I wonder how Liza was doing? I mean, it came to my head, so I must be. She was my best friend. I couldn't believe I was using the word "was." Everything happened so quickly.

I couldn't dwell on it any longer. I now had something to keep my mind occupied. I squeezed the drive in my fist to remind me of that. I now had access to the Dark Web.

I made it to the house and walked in the door, fully expecting to go straight to my room to get started. My mom had other plans. She was slinging her purse over her shoulder.

"Where are you going, Mom?" I asked.

"We're *both* going," she replied. "Detective Harrison asked if we could stop by the police station. He wants to ask us a few questions."

"Oh my God!" I let out. "They figured out it was Travis? We can't go, Mom! We have to get out of here. We'll move away. They won't..,"

"It's about Sabrina's case," my mom jumped in, bringing me back down.

"Oh. Then, does it have to be now?" I questioned defiantly.

"I told him we'd go as soon as you got home from school."

Why, Mom, Why?

I huffed and shook my head.

"Fine. Can I pee first?"

Chapter 39

Mind Games

We sat on the hard wooden bench in the hallway outside the detective bureau on the second floor of the police station. My mom calmly leaned back against the backrest with her purse resting on her lap. I sat upright, my butt barely on the first two slats, biting my pinky nail. Against the wall in front of us was a glass cabinet filled with nostalgic police paraphernalia that held my attention. I particularly liked the display of badges from years past. I wasn't a fan of the bulky hats, though.

The door to the bureau creaked open, and I quickly dropped my hand to my lap, wiping the saliva off my pinky. A sharp edge scraped across my pants, letting me know my nail-biting job was hardly complete. I rubbed my thumb across its jagged edge and silently groaned. That was going to annoy me. Luckily, there were other distractions to keep me from cursing my insufficient manicuring skills, such as Detective Harrison's handsome features poking out from behind the door to greet us.

"Erin, Emma," he nodded and smiled. "I'm glad you could make it."

He extended his hand to my mom as she stood, but I quickly intervened and shook it. If he thought he could make a move on her while I was around, he was sorely mistaken. He gracefully took it in stride and gestured with a slight head tilt and a charismatic grin.

"Please, come in." He swung the door open to allow us a glimpse into his secret lair.

It was a large open room with only three desks furnishing the main floor, barely occupying a third of the space. An out-of-shape, balding man sat at the desk against the wall to our left, pecking at his keyboard with heavy fingers. To the right, at the desk closest to the front wall, another detective, maybe in his mid-fifties, sat forward in his chair, his head propped up between his thumb and first two fingers while he stared at a document at the edge of his desk. The desk in front of his, currently housing an empty chair, I assumed to be Detective Harrison's. The middle of the room was wide open, which made it a little uncomfortable as Detective Harrison escorted us to his desk. As we skitted across the floor, the other men remained professional, never taking their attention away from their duties.

When we arrived at his desk, he had a single guest chair positioned at the front of it. He looked a bit embarrassed as he swung himself around, searching for another. His gaze stopped on his nearest neighbor's chair.

"Ah, here we go," he said, swiping the vacant chair from the other detective's desk and swinging it around to his. "Please, have a seat."

My mom said, "Thank you," and slid to the farther chair. I didn't say anything - just sat in the chair Detective Harrison retrieved and watched him smooth out his tie as he took his seat across from us.

"First, I'd like to apologize for calling you in on such short notice," he began. "I appreciate you taking the time. I know we all have busy lives."

His voice was soft and smooth, which made his apology sound sincere. It also made my heart melt, which made it difficult to be upset with him for asking us here in the first place.

"Now, the reason I asked you here," he continued, sliding his chair closer to his desk so he could rest his elbows on it. "I'd like to ask you some questions about Liza Faraday."

My heart skipped a beat at the mention of her name, and my leg started bouncing again.

"Liza?" I questioned.

"That's right," he replied. "I spoke with another student recently, and they mentioned that Liza and Sabrina were secretly dating. Do you happen to recall seeing the two girls hanging out together or perhaps hearing rumors of a possible relationship?"

"Well, if it was 'secretly dating,'" I answered, "wouldn't me knowing about it defeat the purpose?"

"So the answer is 'no' then?"

"I mean, I don't even think they liked each other. They were completely different. And Sabrina, well, she wasn't the easiest to get along with. I learned that my first week here."

"Oh, really? And how is that?"

"Um...," I tilted my head down and began nervously rubbing the rough edge of my pinky nail again. "You know, just normal mean girl bullying type stuff."

"I see," he responded.

"If you want to know if they were seeing each other," I said, quickly bringing the subject back to the case, "why don't you just ask Liza?"

"Oh, I did," he replied. "She was here earlier today. I told Liza's mother that it could wait until after school, but she offered to bring her right away."

That explains why Liza wasn't in school, I thought.

"So then, you already know the answer," I stated.

My mom lightly tapped my bouncing knee.

"Emma, stop being rude," she said

"It's quite all right, Erin," Detective Harrison said, putting his hand up. "I *did* get an answer from Liza. She denied any relationship with Sabrina."

"There you go then," I retorted.

"Here's the thing, though," he continued. "If they *were* secretly dating, then, as you mentioned, wouldn't telling me the truth 'defeat the purpose'?"

I see what you did there - good one.

I shrugged my shoulders. "Anyway, I don't know anything about it."

He stared at me for a moment. It was a bit uncomfortable. Not for me, but I imagined it must have been for my mom to have to watch him lust after me with those eyes of his. Then he continued.

"Okay. Can we talk about Jill Wells?"

"What about her?"

Bitch.

"How close was she with Sabrina?"

Oh my God! Did he suspect Jill? Did she go back that night and kill Sabrina?

"They were inseparable," I answered. "They were always together. I'd say best friends."

"And yet, even Sabrina's best friend seemed shocked when I asked her about Liza and Sabrina."

"Well then, maybe there *was* no relationship. Maybe that other student lied."

He nodded slightly. "Maybe."

Then silence struck again as I twiddled my thumbs.

"Well, that's all I have," the detective stated, standing from his chair.

My mom and I rose together.

"See? Painless," he said, extending his hand more noticeably toward my mom this time. "Erin, good seeing you again." She shook his hand. Then he extended it to me. "Emma, thank you." I obliged.

I'm pretty sure he just wanted to hold my hand again. Then, my mom did the unthinkable and tried to embarrass me.

"May I use your bathroom?"

Detective Harrison dropped my hand and pointed to the far corner.

"Oh, sure. It's right over there."

"Thank you," my mom said before walking away.

I impatiently started tapping my foot on the floor while staring at the detective. After a few seconds, I flashed him a smile.

He looked at me confusedly. "Is.., is there something amusing, Emma?"

"Why didn't you ask about Patti Lynn?" I inquired. "You asked about Liza. You asked about Jill. Why not Patti?"

"Why would I ask about Patti?" he replied.

"It's just that.., I know the other student was Patti Lynn. She told me you questioned her."

"Okay."

"You should know she makes up stories a lot."

"I've heard," he responded.

"Like, she claimed she confessed to being at the scene of the crime the night of Sabrina's murder."

I watched for his reaction. He didn't flinch.

"And if she had?" the detective questioned.

"Well then, wouldn't you still be questioning her or have her in custody or something? Unless..,"

"Unless, what?" he inquired.

"Unless you've ruled her out as a suspect. And if she's not a suspect, even after confessing her whereabouts that night, then you must have some evidence clearing her."

"You're a smart kid," he responded.

Kid? Kid? I'm eighteen.

"I aced my Law and Justice class," I said with a cocky smile.

"That's great, Emma."

"So.., are you going to fill me in on the evidence?"

He chuckled. "No, I'm not."

"Aw, come on," I said, using my best pouty face. "You're not holding *me* for further questioning either, which means I'm *also* not a suspect. Shouldn't I know what evidence cleared me?"

"You're too much." He said. "I'm sorry, but..,"

I fluttered my eyelids and poured on the overwhelmingly depressed teenage girl look.

"You know what?" he said. "Maybe you *can* help with something."

He bent over, reached into his bottom drawer, and pulled out a couple of manila folders. I wanted to think it was my undeniably pitiful look that did it, but I knew better. He wouldn't freely divulge evidence in an ongoing investigation unless it was an attempt to get a reaction out of me. I knew how to keep my cool (*said the girl who couldn't wait to get back to biting her fingernail*).

Detective Harrison opened one folder, then closed it and put it down. He opened the second folder, pulled a picture from it, and placed it in front of me on the desk. I hadn't noticed it, as my eyes were drawn to the first folder. A picture had slid partially out of it when he put it down. He immediately noticed my curiosity and quickly shuffled the picture back into the folder.

"Was that the body found at the treatment plant? It's been all over the news. Are the two murders related?"

"I can't get into that, Emma. But please, can you tell me if you recognize that?" He pointed at the picture in front of me. I calmly looked down, crossed my arms, crinkled my nose, and shook my head.

"No," I answered, looking back at him.

"Are you sure? Take another look."

I'd seen this ploy a thousand times in detective movies. It wasn't going to work. I glanced down a second time, tilted my head sideways as if seeing it from a different angle might somehow jog a memory, and then looked up again.

"Nope, sorry. I haven't seen that before."

Just then, my mom stepped out of the bathroom. Detective Harrison quickly scooped up the picture and slid it into the manila folder.

"I love that soap in there," my mom said, sniffing her palm as she joined us. "Ready to go, kiddo?"

Again with the kid stuff?

"Thank you again for coming," the detective said. "I'll walk you to the door."

"Of course," my mom answered.

We walked across the floor to the exit. Detective Harrison held the door for us. As we stepped by him into the hallway, he made a final remark.

"Thank you, Emma. Remember, if you think of anything else – anything at all, don't hesitate to contact me. You have my card."

I nodded.

"Goodbye now," he put his hand up in a wave.

We started down the stairs to leave while my mom spouted something about him being a nice man. I don't know; it was something like that. I wasn't really paying attention. My thoughts were on the picture he showed me. It was the murder weapon: a knife covered in blood.

Sabrina's blood.

The knife had a black handle with a gold ring around it.

Shit!

Liza's knife.

Chapter 40

Discovery

It wasn't her. It wasn't her. It wasn't her. No matter how many times I repeated it, the opposite kept flashing in my head. Maybe it *was* her. The murder weapon.., that knife.., it was Liza's. It was just as she described it to me. But what if it wasn't her? She said she lost the knife. What if someone else found it and used it to kill Sabrina? I mean, it was plausible. Wasn't it? Maybe if this were one of those cheesy YA thriller novels. But it wasn't; this was real life. Why else would Liza be so determined to find the knife, dragging me out there to help her search for it? She wanted to get rid of the evidence. But the police already had it. That's why we never found it. She already told me her fingerprints were all over it. It made sense why Patti and I weren't suspects. But the police didn't

251

know whose prints they were. They didn't have Liza's on file.

Wait! Hold on! Why had I been so quick to slap a guilty verdict on Liza? *I don't know, maybe because she'd been acting so strange lately?* That wasn't fair. Detective Harrison asked about Jill, too. I bet *her* prints aren't in the system, either. Was it too hard to believe that Liza was telling the truth about losing the knife? Maybe Jill saw Sabrina walking back to the building, and then, after dropping Trina and Beverly off, she returned to the scene to confront Sabrina, found the knife, and then stabbed her with it. Her best friend? But why? Jealousy? No. Hatred? Possibly. She certainly expressed to me her feelings about gays. If she decided to go back to pick up Sabrina and eavesdropped on her and Liza's conversation..,

She *did* say Sabrina betrayed her. Could she have been *that* mad, though, to stab her best friend? Right. This coming from the girl who, only moments ago, was so eager to stab her own best friend in the back.

She was, I thought. *Past tense. Liza WAS my best friend. Not anymore.*

Still, there was a big difference between figurative and literal stabbing. I didn't know what to think anymore. But then my phone buzzed, making it so I didn't have to think about any of it. It was another message from my secret admirer.

I'll kill, kill, kill you. Just wait.

That was it; I'd had enough. All of this crazy shit kept happening to me, and I wasn't going to let it happen anymore. Carla Wittell – your days of harassing me are numbered.

I sat up with my legs crossed on my bed and opened my laptop. I reached into my pants pocket and dug out the thumb drive Chris had given me. I plugged it in and clicked on the USB drive. The program loaded - something called SparkWeb. Of course, it was. What better way to access the Dark Web than with SparkWeb?

I opened up my browser and stared at the flashing cursor in the prompt bar. It was practically daring me to type. How could I resist such a tempting invitation? *Because people weren't supposed to be fooling around with this crap.* Hell with it - you only live once.

I typed in the dreaded words "Dark Web." At first, nothing happened. Then, my screen flashed, went black, and white text appeared with a blinking white cursor at the top.

Okay. That wasn't so scary. Here we go. I typed in Carla's name and..,

That couldn't be right. "No matches found" flashed on the screen. There had to be something. Did I do something wrong? I typed the name again and hit enter. And again, no results. I felt my insides boil. Every muscle within me was tightening. How? Why? Why can't anything go right? I wanted to throw the laptop across the room.

Calm down. Relax.

I closed my eyes, took a deep breath, and exhaled.

There, wasn't that better?

NO! Whatever. I yanked Chris' thumb drive from the USB port, closed my laptop, and slid it to the side. I was kicking and screaming like a baby on the inside. I squeezed the thumb drive in my fist one more time for good measure. Take that, SparkWeb!

I shook my head and let out a little giggle. I had to find the humor in it, or I'd go crazy. Well, that was it. I tried; I failed. All I could do was give the thumb drive back. I grabbed my backpack from the floor and pulled it onto the bed. I unzipped the front pocket to toss the drive into, and I spotted the crumpled paper I'd thrown in there the day before.

Liza's note.

I had forgotten all about it. I pulled the balled-up wad from the pocket and unraveled it, trying to smooth out the wrinkles with my palm. The numerous creases didn't make it easy, but I read the words. Time stopped for a second until I could catch my breath, and then it resumed.

"Oh no," I gasped. "Liza. What did you do?"

I closed my eyes and wondered if it could be true. Of course, it was true. Somewhere, deep inside, I always knew. Just like I now knew what I had to do. I glanced over at the laptop and pulled it toward me. I lifted the screen, looked at the thumb drive still in my hand, and plugged it back in.

Chapter 41

Suffer the Children

How could I sit here and pretend I didn't know? Who was I kidding? I did that all the time. It was my specialty. My entire teenage years were filled with others' secrets I pretended to know nothing about. But this was different. This secret involved someone I cared about. Someone who I thought cared about me.

I looked at Liza beside me in homeroom, her black hoodie shrouding most of her face from me like she couldn't stand the look of me. How did things end up this way? I thought about what she meant to me over the past six months. She'd been there for me. We had each other's backs. She was there for me during my first week when Sabrina.., well, she was my best friend.

I didn't know for sure if I could do it. It wasn't something I wanted to do. But maybe.., maybe something I *needed* to do. I wasn't even sure if I'd make it to school this morning. I was so nauseous. At least talking with my mom helped.

"You're looking ragged this morning?" my mom stated as I stumbled into the kitchen. "Did you not sleep well?"

"Not really, no," I replied.

"Bad dreams?"

My silence answered her question easier than any words could.

"Okay, then," she said, buttering some toast. "Did you want to talk about it?"

"Mom! I'm fine." I spoke louder than I meant to.

She threw her hands up defensively in front of her chest. "Okay, Miss snappy-pants. Forget I asked."

She cut the two pieces of toast from corner to corner – the way I liked it, and placed them on a plate in front of me.

"It's just..,"

Arrr, she did it. How did she always get me to talk?

"I'm listening," she said, placing the butter knife on a paper towel and leaning her arms on the center island to give me her full attention.

"If you knew someone did something bad – like, really bad..,"

"Like kill a man in their basement and cover it up, bad?" she half-joked.

"I'm already feeling sick, Mom. You don't have to make it worse."

"Okay, I'm sorry, honey," she said, reaching forward and rubbing my forearm. "Go on."

"I think I might know who killed Sabrina."

"You think you might?"

"I mean, I do. Maybe. Probably."

"You don't sound very confident."

"I am. It's just..,"

"You know them personally, and you don't want to be the one responsible for getting them arrested."

I didn't answer her. I just looked down at my plate and nodded.

"Emma, after what we did.., what I did, I'm probably not the best person to tell you what the right thing to do is. Only you can make that decision."

"But it's hard, Mom."

"I know. And I can see you're struggling with this. Is it a teacher, a student?"

"A student," I replied.

"Have you thought about talking with them - asking them if what you believe is true? Maybe they didn't do it. Or, if they did.., maybe you can convince them to turn themselves in. Or, you know, do nothing and let the police handle it."

"That's just it, Mom," I responded. "I'm not sure the police will figure it out without a little push in the right direction."

"Emma, it's what they do."

"Let's hope not, for our sake, with the Travis situation."

I saw my mom's shoulders drop from the harsh reminder, and she let out a saddened breath.

"But really, if they don't have enough evidence, they might not be able to act on it. And then Sabrina's death will.., and her parents.., well, she'll never get justice."

"Emma, honey, calm down. It sounds to me like you've already made a decision."

"I haven't. I still don't want any of this to be true."

"Just because you don't want something to be true doesn't mean it isn't."

"I know."

"Listen – give yourself the day to think about it. When you get home, if you decide you want to share what you know, we can contact Detective Harrison, and you can let him handle it from there. If you decide you want to forget the whole thing, we can do that, too. Fair?"

I nodded. "Yeah."

"Good. Now eat your toast before you're late for school."

She didn't solve my moral dilemma as I hoped she would *(as if we even followed some moral code after what we did)*, but it made me feel better to know she supported whatever decision I made. Maybe I *should* confront Liza as my mom suggested. At this point, it couldn't hurt.

I leaned my head sideways to get closer to her.

"Liza," I whispered. "Can we talk?"

She turned her head slightly, just enough for her left eye to show beyond the front of her hood.

"Did you say something?" she whispered back.

"Yeah. I need to ask you something, and I want you to tell me the truth."

"What is it?" she asked.

She pulled her hoodie back off her head, and that was when I saw her swollen cheek and the bruise under her eye.

"What happened to you?" I asked, feeling concerned as if she were still the best friend I wanted her to be.

"Oh, this?" she replied, pointing to her face. "This is what you get when your seriously messed-up mom thinks she can beat you into becoming straight."

"I thought she didn't know."

"She didn't. Not until we got called into the police station yesterday to answer questions. That detective guy asked me if Sabrina and I were dating. Somebody must have told him. I think we *both* know who that was. You should have seen my mom's face when she heard that."

"What did you say?"

"I denied it. I couldn't let my mom know - not like that, anyway. Plus, how would that have made me look? I was dating the girl who got killed."

"But if you denied it, then why did your mom beat you?"

"I think that was her way of warning me. I still don't think she knows. Or maybe she's in denial herself. Basically, she doesn't like the idea of me being with *anyone*."

"That sucks."

"I'm used to it. What did you want to ask me?"

"I..,"

The bell rang, interrupting my thoughts.

"I'll talk with you later," I said.

Liza pulled her hoodie back over her head, grabbed her bag, and walked away. I sat for a few seconds, unable to get my legs to respond. Liza didn't deserve to get beaten. She didn't deserve to get stuck with the mother she had. She didn't deserve all the..,

My thoughts switched gears.

Sabrina didn't deserve to die. Her mom didn't deserve to lose her daughter.

Shit! Shit!

This *all* sucked.

Chapter 42

Confrontation

The day was flying by, and I still hadn't decided what I was going to do. Maybe that was the answer. "Do nothing." That was still an option. I wasn't a cop. It wasn't my job to solve crimes. I should let Detective Harrison earn his pay. Sure, I could turn a blind eye to the whole thing. That would be so easy. I was graduating in less than two weeks. After that, I wouldn't have to see any of these.., what are they called around here? Massholes.

I'd already planned to attend college back in my home state. I'd wanted to go to Penn since I was eleven. Why should I care about what did or didn't happen to my classmates here? Only.., about some things, I cared a lot. As much as I liked holding onto secrets and learning about everybody's dirty laundry, it didn't make me a horrible person.

Of course not; you're just always put in horrible positions.

Those thoughts weren't helping. I needed to have that talk with Liza. Gym class was my last chance. I'd get her to open up. She'd tell me the truth. Then we could work out a plan together. She could come clean to Detective Harrison. I'd be with her every step of the way. That's what best friends do for each other. I wouldn't let her down. I'd help her make the right decision.

I sat with my legs on either side of the locker room bench, staring at Carla's name. I'd written it on a sheet of paper while I waited for Liza to arrive. It wasn't working. I couldn't focus on that when I was about to confront Liza. It was just as well, I suppose. It would only frustrate me, anyway, and I wouldn't want that to affect how my conversation went. The funny thing was, I was so focused on how I *couldn't* focus that I didn't hear Liza come up behind me until she was peering over my shoulder and breathing down my neck.

"Who's Clara?" she questioned.

"It's *Carla*," I replied. Not Clar..,"

And then it hit me like a ton of bricks. It couldn't be that simple, could it? *Thanks, Liza.*

I reached back into my bag, grabbed my pen, and rewrote the name, rearranging some letters until..,

Fuck me!

Carla Wittell was Clara Willett.

Now, *that* was a name I couldn't forget. It was staring me in the face the whole time. It wasn't even that clever. How could I not see it? It all made sense now.

"Okay, so who is she?" Liza persisted, throwing her gym bag on the floor by an open locker.

I quickly crumpled the paper and spun to face her.

"It's no one. Don't worry about it." *Real smooth, Emma.*

Liza sat beside me, changing out of her black, calf-high boots into her sneakers. I figured it was now or never.

"Liza, I wanted to..,"

"No, wait," Liza interrupted. "I have something I want to say first."

"Okay."

"I want to apologize for the way I've been acting lately. I shouldn't have been so hard on you. It was just.., with Sabrina's death and everything, it hit me hard. And the way she acted like she never cared for me.., it just really hurt me. You know?"

"Liza, I get it. It's fine."

"No, it's not. I've been a total bitch to you."

I couldn't argue there, I thought.

"I was angry with everyone," she continued while tying her shoe. "Especially Jill. Sabrina used to tell me how Jill was such a homophobe. That's why she was afraid to come out. She thought it would cause a rift between them, and she might lose her spot on the cheerleading team. That's why I left that note for her. I knew she'd burn her own bridge if someone handed her a match."

"Wait, wait," I stopped her. "What are you talking about? What note?"

"Oh, um..," she hesitated, biting her lower lip. "I kinda slipped a note into Jill's locker, telling her about me and Sabrina seeing each other."

"You 'kinda slipped'? It was *you* who told Jill that Sabrina was gay? You straight up blamed me for it the other day."

"I know, and I'm sorry. That's why I'm telling you now. I didn't want you to know it was me. But look. I was right. Jill told her friends and started badmouthing Sabrina, and look at her now. She's no longer Miss Popular. Everybody sees her for who she really is."

"I don't believe this," I said heatedly. "What's the matter with you? You even had me blaming Patti for it."

"So what? Who cares? It's just Patti. She'll get over it."

"I can't believe you just said that. Patti's been nothing but sweet to you. She's annoying some-times, but she only wants to be your friend."

"Give me a break," Liza responded, standing and holding the second boot she'd removed. "Why would I want someone like her to be my friend? She's such a nerd."

I held my tongue. There was that thing I *wanted* to say but thought against it, and then there was the thing I *did* say.

"You know what? Why would I want someone like *you* to be *my* friend?"

"Really?" she said in a snotty voice. "Just like that? That's how easy it is for you? If that's the way you want it to be, then you can forget I even apologized to you." She shook her head and curled her upper lip. "I thought you were different."

She threw her boot onto her open bag and stormed out of the locker room into the gymnasium, leaving me to dwell on her words. I couldn't believe she was like that. I'd never seen that side of her before. She had me fooled the entire time. I thought I was good at hiding the lies, but Liza was the queen of it. I shook my head in disgust. All of that, and I never got a chance to ask her about the murder. If I had any doubts before.., I wouldn't put it past her now.

I leaned my head forward into my palm. My eyes glanced over at Liza's bag. Where her boot had landed, her phone peeked out from under one of the bag's top flaps. I stared at it as thoughts swirled around my head. I looked at the gym door. I stared at the phone again. I closed my eyes and thought hard about what I should do. I didn't have to think long. I knew.

I opened my eyes and reached for my backpack.

Chapter 43

Blame Game

With a heavy heart, I walked into the house, the sadness of my decision displayed on my face. My dilemma was no more. I'd taken steps to rectify a wrong, and I'd take a few more to make things right. It had to be done, and like it or not, I had to be the one to do it. Liza certainly wasn't going to cooperate.

My mom heard the door shut and came strolling from the kitchen. She could tell right away from my expression I was dealing with a lot. Maybe too much. She extended her arms.

"Oh, honey." She wrapped her arms around me in a hug and rested her cheek on the top of my head. I wasn't a soft girl, but I fully welcomed the embrace.

"Mom..,"

"Shhhh. It's okay. I know it's not easy. You can still change your mind if you'd like. I won't look at you any differently."

"No, I have to do this. I *want* to do this. For Sabrina. And for all the other girls at school."

And also.., for myself.

My mom pulled away from me and held my upper arms, looking into my eyes.

"You are a brave girl. You hear me? And you're doing the right thing. I'm very proud of you."

"None of that is going to make this any easier."

"I know. But I'll be with you."

"Do you still have Detective Harrison's card?" I asked.

She pressed her lips together to form a sorrowful grin and nodded. She rubbed my upper arms to soothe me, forced the ends of her lips to curl higher, and then walked away to get it. I exhaled heavily, letting the pent-up stress leave me.

Hold it together, I thought. *You can do this, Emma. Remember why you're doing this.*

My mom came back with the card.

⧖ ⧖ ⧖

"Emma, come on in," Detective Harrison said with a kind smile. "Hello, Erin." He nodded and stepped aside for us to enter the bureau office.

We knew the way to his desk and marched on in. He followed behind. I grabbed the chair at the front of his desk, but he stopped me before I could sit.

"Not there today," he stated. "This way." He nodded to a door in the corner.

We followed him through the door and into a hallway, where he pointed to another door on the right.

"This one here," he said, opening it for us.

It was a small room with a rectangular table in the middle with three chairs around it. It reminded me of the interrogation rooms you see in the cop shows. Except for no mirror on the wall. Was that what this was? Was I about to be interrogated?

"Please, have a seat," he said, waving an open hand to the two chairs closest to us. He walked around to the lone chair on the opposite side. "I understand you'd like to make a statement, Emma."

I nervously nodded at first but then spoke up. "Yes. I mean, um, yeah, I would."

"Okay." He pulled his phone from his jacket pocket, looked at the screen, then looked at me. "I hope you don't mind me recording this." He said it in a way that made me feel I had a choice when I knew I didn't. He was sweet like that.

I shook my head.

He smiled. "Great." His thumb hit the record button, and he placed the phone on the table in front of him. He sat silently for a few seconds, watching me stare at his phone. Then, he began. "So, Emma, can you tell me what this is about?"

I felt my mom's hand lightly rub my back for encouragement.

"I know who killed Sabrina Beaulieu," I said.

The detective's face turned serious.

"That's a big claim," he responded. "May I ask..,"

"I lied to you yesterday," I interjected.

"About..?"

"The knife. I know whose knife it is."

My mom sat forward. "What knife?"

"You don't know about it, Mom," I replied. "You were in the bathroom."

The detective jumped in. "Whose knife is it, Emma, and how do you know?"

"It belongs to..," I hesitated, wondering if I was doing the right thing. I was. "It belongs to Liza Faraday. She told me about it."

"She told you about killing Sabrina?" he questioned.

"No, she told me about the knife. She described it to me. It was the one in the photo you showed me."

"I don't understand. Why was Liza describing a knife to you?"

"Because she asked me to help her find it."

"What?" My mother blurted. "When was this?"

"That night you drove me into town to meet her."

"You told me you two were just hanging out and talking."

"Mom, will you let me speak?" I said louder than I should have.

She looked at Detective Harrison, "I'm sorry."

"It's okay," he assured her. "So, Emma, Liza asked if you could help look for her knife. And this was where exactly?"

"Outside of the old mill building."

"The mill building where Sabrina Beaulieu was killed?" he questioned.

"Yes."

"Are you saying Liza was there the night of Sabrina's murder?"

I nodded.

He pointed to his phone to remind me recordings didn't pick up head nods.

"Yes," I replied.

"Did she tell you this?"

"Yes."

"Did she tell you why she was there?"

"She said she wanted to talk with Sabrina. They had fought earlier, and she wanted to work things out."

"But she brought a knife with her," Detective Harrison pointed out.

"She said she only brought it for protection in case there were vagrants or creeps or something."

"And you believed her?"

"I mean, she's my.., she *was* my best friend."

He breathed out and displayed a skeptical grin. "Okay. So Liza goes to meet Sabrina - she brings a knife with her for protection - then what?"

"Well, she said she talked with Sabrina – well, fought again, I guess, and then went to leave, but she tripped out the door, and that was when she must have dropped the knife."

"The knife she later asked you to help her find."

"Yes."

"And knowing a classmate was killed at that building didn't make you question any of this?" he asked.

"I did, actually, but when she explained it all to me.., she made it sound convincing."

"But now you're not so convinced?" he questioned. "After she isn't your best friend anymore?"

"No, it's not like that," I replied. "When you showed me the bloody knife, I recognized it right away. It was exactly as she described. She told me she didn't do anything, but the blood.., I bet you'll find her prints on it, too."

"So Liza had the knife, but she never actually *told* you she killed Sabrina, is that correct?"

"No, but..,"

"But, what?"

I reached into my pocket and pulled out a crumpled piece of paper.

"I caught her writing this note before she threw it in the trash."

I handed Detective Harrison the wrinkled paper. He stared at it for a few seconds, and then, to get it on recording, he read it allowed.

"Mrs. Beaulieu, it's my fault your daughter is dead."

"You'll find that's her handwriting," I added.

"Why come forward with this now, Emma?"

I looked at my mom and then back to the detective. "I wanted to do the right thing."

"Well, I appreciate you sharing this with me, Emma. It certainly doesn't paint Liza in a good light, but it doesn't prove she killed anybody either. But it will, however, allow us to bring her in here for further questioning."

"There's more," I said.

"More? Okay, go on."

"After the note and the bloody knife, I started to think that Liza might have actually done it. You know, killed Sabrina. During gym today, she left her phone sitting on her bag in the locker room. I shouldn't have done it, but I checked her text messages. I think I was maybe hoping to find something that would prove her innocence. Instead..,"

"Instead, what, Emma?" the detective asked.

"I think you should see them for yourself," I replied. "She sent quite a few threatening messages to Sabrina. Some of them are.., really bad."

"I see. Can you give me an example?"

"Just that, well, she mentions killing her. More than once,"

Detective Harrison exhaled heavily. "Very well. Is there anything else you'd like to share?"

"Just.., I hope this can bring peace to Sabrina's parents."

"I think they'd appreciate that," he nodded. "We'll definitely get Liza back in here to see what she has to say. This new information should be enough to get a judge to sign off on a search warrant for Liza's phone."

Detective Harrison hit the stop button on the recording.

"I think I have everything I need for now. I appreciate you coming in today, Emma. It must have been very difficult for you. You're very brave."

"I told her that, too," my mom said proudly, sitting up in her chair.

"Depending on what we learn, I may need you to come back in to answer more questions."

"I understand," I answered.

"Good. Then, if there's nothing more, I'll walk you two out."

My mom and I stood as he waved us into the hall. He led us back through the main office space and to the exit.

At the door, I turned and extended my hand.

He smiled and reciprocated.

While we shook, I smiled at him and rubbed my thumb back and forth along the back of his hand. He looked down at our hands and then back into my eyes. I licked my lips to give him a hint of my intentions. He knew. He offered a smile. My mom saw my flirtatious gesture and cleared her throat.

"Eh hmm. Emma." She gave me a stern glare. "Shall we go?"

I released the detective's hand and put my head down as I walked by my mom.

"Thank you so much, Detective Harrison."

"Thank you, Erin. I'll be in touch."

I could only hope he'd touch me, I thought. *Maybe someday.*

Well, that was it. I did it. Now, I sit back and see what happens.

Chapter 44

A Fitting End

The chair was empty, and it was my doing. It wasn't the only vacant seat, but it was the one beside me, so it had my attention. Unlike me, the band played on without care or distraction. Patti sat two rows in front of me beside the other chair that lay empty except for a bouquet of white roses that sat upon it. She turned and looked over her shoulder in my direction, her yellow tassel dangling from side to side. She smiled and waved. I put up my hand as a kind gesture and did my best to smile back. I glanced to my left into the crowd of proud parents and invited guests, their phones held high, taking pictures to share with the world on social media. My mom was among them, snapping instant memories and whistling and waving.

I brushed a black ball of lint from my white gown and watched it flitter to the ground beside my shoe, the name Liza written in black marker just below the laces. I looked at the empty chair again, and my thoughts wandered back to my first week at Bellamy High.

I heard the other girls snickering as soon as I turned off the shower. They seemed like a fun bunch of girls. I'd make friends with them in no time. I stepped from the shower stall and wrapped a towel around myself, squeezing the excess water from my hair with my hands before walking out into the gym locker area. The four girls present, all wearing cheerleader uniforms, curbed their laughter and stiffened when they saw me.

They were on the bench, huddled around an open locker near the showers. I flashed an awkward smile as I walked by them. "Hi."

They didn't respond, only peered at me with unpleasant glances. I heard the tall one whisper, "Wait for it." The others burst out in hushed laughter. I continued to the opposite bench, where my duffle bag was. I noticed immediately that the top was only half-zipped. I didn't think much of it, though, until I opened it the rest of the way to get my clothes. I laid them out on the bench and shuffled through them, searching for my underwear.

Shirt, bra, socks, yoga pants, sneakers. No underwear. I dug back into my bag, thinking I'd missed them. No luck. I turned to the other girls, their wide-eyed stares upon me.

"Did any of you find a pair of underwear on the floor? I think I dropped mine."

The tall one replied, serious-faced, "Dropped them? Is that your story?"

One of the other girls who sat beside her tried to contain her laughter, making snorting sounds through her nose. I looked at her curiously and politely grinned.

"What do you mean?" I asked.

"You think we don't know what you did?" the tall one replied. "No wonder you were taking a shower. You just couldn't hold it, huh?"

I shook my head, confused. "What are you talking about?"

"Don't play dumb," the blonde continued. "We know what you did." She pointed to the toilet stalls along the side wall.

They couldn't have been more obvious with their snickering. Curiosity got the best of me. I walked over and opened the first stall; it was empty.

I opened the second stall, and my heart sank. I felt my face scrunch in disgust. My underwear was floating in the toilet bowl where someone had taken a dump and didn't flush. The brown water and solid waste mingled with the silk panties.

I stormed back to the cheerleaders, my teeth clenched tight.

"That wasn't funny," I seethed.

"What are you talking about?" The tall one questioned.

"You know what I'm talking about. One of you threw my underwear in the toilet."

"Don't blame us because you shit your pants," the same girl replied. "We were just sitting here chatting."

"Yeah, right," I said. "And I suppose my bag unzipped itself, too."

"I've heard of that happening. It's a strange phenomenon."

"You're a real bitch," I shouted.

At that, the girl stood up threateningly. She was four or five inches taller than me.

"You know, we were going to keep your disgusting secret to ourselves," she said, "but now, I think we'll let everyone else know the new girl shit her pants."

One of the other girls egged her on.

"Get her, Sabrina."

Now I know your name, bitch, I thought. Do your worst.

She might have. For all the bravado displayed on my face, I was standing in a towel, using one hand to keep it from unraveling. My feet were still wet from the water dripping down my legs; if I tried to kick, I'd likely slip and crack my head open on the floor. That left me with one hand to defend myself. Luckily, I didn't have to, as Liza, the girl I'd met the day before, walked through the door.

She looked tough in her black makeup, wearing a jean jacket, short leather skirt, black boots, and torn black fishnet stockings. Sabrina backed down as if the two of them had a bad history.

"What's going on, you guys?" she asked, the four girls' faces telling a good part of the story.

I spoke right up. "This tall, skinny bitch threw my underwear in the toilet with shit in it."

"That sucks," she said. "Do you have another pair?"

"No. Why would I have another pair?"

"Right," she replied. She looked at Sabrina, shook her head, then looked at the other three girls. Then, without a thought, she reached up under her skirt, pulled her underwear down around her ankles, and stepped out of the leg holes. She bent down, picked up the undies, and dangled them between her fingers for the four girls. With a smirk on her face, she walked over to the stall where my underwear was and threw hers in with mine. Then she flushed the toilet.

When she walked back, she glared at the cheerleaders, their mouths open as they gawked at her actions. She glanced over at my clothes on the bench. Then she turned to me and winked.

"Just think how great your ass is going to look in those yoga pants."

That was the beginning of what I thought was a beautiful relationship. I never thought it would end the way it had. We were supposed to be graduating together. Instead, she was being held without bail, awaiting trial.

I placed my palm on the empty seat beside me. Why did you do it, Liza? Worse, why didn't you come forward afterward instead of making me do what I had to do? Do you think I wanted to do that? They probably wouldn't have been able to figure it out if it wasn't for me. But it was *your* fault. You left your phone right there in your bag. What was I supposed to do? I couldn't let Sabrina's death go unsolved. The police didn't have enough evidence. They needed more. So I gave them more.

That cloning software Chris directed me to had worked better than I'd hoped. I was able to push texts to Liza's phone and manipulate the dates and times. It let me enter the sender and recipient information, and I got to choose which messages to clone. I made sure to choose the right ones.

```
I should kill you for what you did to me.
And soon, you'll pay.
You'll pay for it all.
If I ever run into you alone somewhere,
you're dead. You hear me? DEAD!
I'll kill, kill, kill you. Just wait.
```

Those, with the note she wrote and the bloody knife, along with mine and Patti's statements, should be enough to prove her guilt. She won't get away with it. I couldn't believe she dared to deny it, screaming at the top of her lungs when they came to pick her up at school. They walked her out in handcuffs right in front of everybody. In the end, it served her right. She got what she deserved. And I..,

Well, I got something out of it too.

Our class valedictorian finished her speech, and the commencement of the diploma ceremony for the graduating class of Bellamy High began. When Principal Malik eventually called my name, the students and attending spectators erupted in cheers. Of the entire graduating class, I received the loudest ovation.

When the ceremony was through, and the students were left to search for the lost caps they'd excitedly tossed into the air, people kept coming up to me to thank me for bringing justice for Sabrina by turning in her killer. My mom did her part, bragging about how wonderful and brave I'd been. Students I hadn't even talked to during my time here suddenly wanted to get to know me. It was as I said a long time ago: it'll take a lot of work on my part, but I'll get them to like me. People always do. There's just something about me; I'm a very likable girl.

I heard a voice call to me from behind.

"Emma!"

I knew who it was right away and shouted my response as I turned to greet her.

"The one and only."

Patti smiled and hugged me. "I'll allow you to use that line this once. After that, I charge a handsome fee."

We separated.

"How are you, Patti?"

"I'm good. Can you believe it; we graduated!"

"We did. We made it through the most awkward years of our lives."

"I don't think I could have done it without you and Li.., I mean, without you."

"You would have. You're stronger than you realize. You'll figure that out next year."

"I know," she replied with a frown. "It's sad that you're leaving to go to college out of state."

"It's something I've always wanted to do. But don't worry, we can stay in touch."

Patti's face lit up. "You mean it?"

"Of course."

Patti hugged me again. "Thanks, Emma. You're my best friend."

I thought about it, remaining silent for a few seconds. Then I caved.

"You're my best friend, too, Patti. Now get off me; you're squeezing the life out of me."

"Oh, sorry," she said, releasing me. "I should go find Chris. There's probably something he wants to ask me." She winked.

"Go get him."

Then I was alone. I turned to see my mom hamming it up with a couple of parents on the sidelines. My eyes drifted to the chair with the roses on it.

Sabrina's chair.

It looked no different than Liza's chair except for the arrangement.

How ironic that the two girls whose journey ended too soon were the two girls who started my unforgettable journey at Bellamy High.

Now, it was over. It was time for the next chapter in my life to begin.

I couldn't wait to see what it had in store for me.

Four Months Later

The Camaro came to a screeching stop inches away from the curb in the side parking lot of the campus. The sign at the front of my car said, "Faculty parking only." They'd let it slide; I wouldn't be there long. I pulled my shades up onto my head and stared out the passenger-side window at the jealous faces gawking at my ride, a reminder I'd been through this before. Only, this time, it wasn't a dream. This time, it was real. *Thanks, Travis*, I thought. *You were finally good for something.*

I couldn't be blamed for his stupid carelessness, leaving his car's title in the glove box like that. What was a girl to do? It's not like he would be needing it. The police never identified his body, and the case went cold. He didn't have anyone who cared about him or would miss him. As far as anyone was concerned, Travis was just another nameless person in a faceless crowd. And since we had to move his car from the airport parking lot anyway, I figured I'd make the most of it. I signed Travis' name on the title and sold myself the car. Or should I say my "uncle" sold me his car? That's what I told Detective Harrison when he came around to thank me for my help. I even let him sit in the car since he was a big fan. Now, I'm a big fan too.

Liza pled her innocence in court. The jury didn't buy it, especially after my testimony. I had to give up a few more secrets that I promised Liza I never would, but the circumstances required it, and I was under oath. Being over eighteen, she was tried as an adult and sentenced to twenty-five years in prison with the possibility of parole after seventeen. I'm sure she'll have forgiven me by then. I've already forgiven her for making me turn her in.

Patti Lynn, "the one and only," or should I say, Patti *Green*, was right about Chris. He proposed to her two days after graduation. It wasn't a long engagement; they got married two months later. I was her Maid of Honor. Actually, I was her *entire* bridesmaid entourage. She was okay with that; I was too.

The break after high school allowed me to do a little research on my crazed stalker, Clara Willett. I knew who she was, and it all made sense after I put it together. She was a classmate from back home in Cameron County Junior/Senior High School. She was a real wiz when it came to electronics and software, so it didn't surprise me to learn it was she who'd somehow disguised her number and identity. When I learned she would be attending Penn State in the fall, my college plans changed. Hey, at least I was going to *some* Penn, even if it wasn't the *real* Penn. I'd already made plans to transfer after my first year.

I'd watched Clara a few times, making her way across Campus on her way to class. It was 11:10 a.m., and like clockwork, she'd arrived, crossing the street onto the campus grounds. I'd made up my mind; today was the day.

I gathered myself and exited the car, admiring myself in the reflection of my driver-side window. I gave myself a wink for encouragement, then dashed across the lawn after Clara.

"Hey, Clara!" I announced when I was almost to her.

She stopped and turned to face me. When she saw who I was, she became skittish, glancing from side to side to see if there were others nearby who could save her if I became violent.

"Emma? Wh-what are you doing here?"

"I'm looking for you," I answered.

She clutched the strap of her backpack with both hands.

"Me?" she questioned nervously.

"Don't play dumb, Clara. I know it's you who's been sending those messages. I want to know why."

"You're not going to kill me, are you?"

I shook my head, confused. "What? Why would I kill you?"

"Because of my texts and because..,"

"First of all," I interrupted, "I'm not a killer. Second of all, if I were, I wouldn't kill the mother of a young child."

Oh yeah, I should probably mention - Clara was the student Mr. Blouth got pregnant.

"Where *is* your kid, anyway?" I asked. "It must be difficult for you, having a baby at home and still managing to go to school."

"She's back home with my mom. I go back twice a week to visit with her."

That wasn't so bad. It was only an hour-and-a-half drive to Gibson.

"I'm trying to make something of myself so we can have a future," she continued.

"I get all of that, but why the threatening messages? What did I ever do to you?"

"Right. Like, you don't know. It's *your* fault I'm stuck raising my child on my own."

"What are you talking about? Do I look like a bear to you?"

"I saw you, Emma. I saw you that night on the trail with Charles. I hid behind a tree up on the embankment overlooking the trail. I overheard you two. I know he was only out there because you asked him to meet with you. And then.., and then I watched you two kiss. He was supposed to leave his wife for me, Emma. *Me*. Not you. I was the one carrying his child. You knew I was pregnant, and you went after Charles behind my back. After you were through with your kisses and your teases, and you left him out there, I confronted him.

"He promised me it was his last time seeing you and that he was committing himself to me. He was leaving his wife. We were going to be a family together. I went back home that night, knowing in my heart that he loved me. And then.., and then he got mauled by that bear. That's on *you*, Emma. He was only out there that night because *you* couldn't stand someone else being more important than you. And because of it, my daughter is growing up without a father."

I didn't know what to say. I didn't know she knew about me and Charles. I also didn't know how to tell her I *was* more important to him than she was. He told me so. But still, he was never going to leave his wife. Clara and I were just two in a long line of students he was fooling around with. I had enough sense to know that, but I was okay with it. I just enjoyed the touch of older men. And Mr. Blouth.., Charles.., was just a perv who liked young high school girls. I guess Clara was more naïve than I thought she was. I could tell her the truth, but there was no sense in it now. The man was dead.

"I'm sorry, Clara. I was going to tell you. But then the bear.., and Mr. Blouth's death.., it didn't matter after that."

"It mattered to *me*," she yelled. "I loved him, and you took him away from me. I'll never forgive you for that."

"So, as payback, you thought it would be fun to send me threatening messages?"

"I wasn't going to do anything," she said. "I was just trying to scare you. It made me feel better."

I felt sorry for this sad, pathetic girl. But I also didn't blame her. She had every right to be mad at me. Not for Charles' death. Some things happen that are beyond our control. But for being a shitty friend. Still, I couldn't let her continue to threaten me, even if it was her way of coping.

"I couldn't care less if it makes you feel better, Clara. The messages have to stop. I know it's you sending them now. I have them all saved. If they continue, I'm going to the police. You can get in a lot of trouble. Not to mention, it'll come out that you were sleeping with Mr. Blouth. How do you think the good folks in Gibson would react to that? Would they ever look at you the same again, knowing you were trying to steal Dr. Meredith Blouth's husband away from her? I'd think long and hard about that if I were you."

"You're a..,"

"Mean bitch," I cut her off. "I know. Test me and find out *how* mean." I turned and walked away. It felt weird. I wasn't really that mean at all, but I needed her to know how serious I was. It was for her sake. I was trying to protect her. I held onto her secret for this long, and I would continue. But if the nasty texts persisted, I'd have no choice but to take action, and the truth would come out. Hopefully, she believed me, and I wouldn't have to worry about it anymore.

I arrived back at my housing unit to find my mom waiting in the lobby.

"Mom, what are you doing here?" I asked.

"Did you forget about our lunch date?"

"Oh, right. That's today. I guess I *did* forget. You're lucky I came back when I did, or you might have been waiting around for a while."

"Then I would have hung around and waited. You think I don't know my daughter? That's why I brought a book with me."

My mom loved her thrillers. She raised the book she was holding, *Just Listen*, by some lame, unknown author, and shook it as if I didn't believe her.

"Besides," she continued, "I haven't seen your room yet."

Tell me that wasn't the biggest hint. I rolled my eyes.

"Come on," I said.

We arrived at my room, a single occupancy with a bedroom the size of a closet, a bathroom only a hobbit could love, and a small area I used as a kitchen that consisted of a mini fridge, a micro-wave, and a desk that doubled as a table. The main room was about the size of the office in our old house, which was to say it was compact.

I watched my mom wander around the space, giving it her full inspection. While she did, my mind drifted back to my earlier meeting with Clara. I really hurt her. But it wasn't my fault, no matter what she believed. I wasn't responsible for Mr. Blouth's death. He didn't have to meet with me. That was his choice. He wanted me. I mean, maybe I shouldn't have been with him, but I enjoyed it too much. Maybe I *wasn't* such a nice girl.

"Emma, what's the matter?" My mom asked.

It must have been written on my face.

"I'm a lousy friend," I replied.

"What? Where did that come from?"

"I had to turn in my best friend, Mom. She trusted me. I mean, I know what Liza did was wrong, stabbing Sabrina five times, lying to me, but..,"

"Six times."

"What?" I questioned.

"Sabrina was stabbed six times," she answered.

I paused my thoughts for a moment, confused at her statement.

"But the police said..,"

"Two of them were in the same spot," she cut in, "though I can understand how they wouldn't have known that."

"But.., h-how would *you* have known that?"

She exhaled through her nose and smirked.

"Oh, come now, Emma. You're not going to stand there and pretend you didn't know."

I felt my lower jaw quiver as I shook my head in disbelief. What was she saying?

"I already told you; do you think I don't know my little girl? I knew you wouldn't call those cheerleaders to cancel that fake party. It's a good thing I left work when I did so I could catch them. Leave it to me to clean up your mess. Again! I'll have you know, I was only going there to apologize to those girls and send them home. I parked on the road and walked to the fence. That was when I heard two girls arguing. Suddenly, the side door flew open and I saw Liza stumble out and fall. She picked herself up and ran in the opposite direction. She never even knew I was there. Then, Sabrina walked out. She was alone, laughing smugly, the heartless bitch. All I could think about was how that girl treated you when you first got to Bellamy. You know I can't stand to see my baby girl hurt. And I wasn't going to let her treat others that way either. So, I stepped into the open and told her I wanted to have a little chat with her. I pointed to the open door; she made her way back inside. I was going to have it out with her – put her in her place. As I followed her to the doorway, my foot kicked a knife. Well, if that wasn't a sign. I didn't know it was Liza's at the time. I pulled my sleeve over my hand, picked up the knife, and held it behind me as I entered. That little whore never saw it coming.

"It's a shame Liza had to take the fall like that, but you had to do what you had to do. As you said, if I went to prison, who would take care of you?"

"Mom.., y-you killed Sabrina?"

"Oh, don't act so surprised. I wouldn't have to do these things if you'd learn to solve your own problems. You need to be more like me. Stronger. That's right. Do you honestly think I wanted to get back together with that no-good son of a bitch, Travis? Of course not. But I wanted him back in my life so I could punish him for what he did to me - to *us*. Sure, I hit a stumbling block when he locked me in the basement, but I wasn't going to let that stop me. He was never going to make it out of Massachusetts alive. I was going to make sure of that."

I felt tears filling my eyes. My body was shaking. I couldn't believe what I was hearing.

"What are you saying," I mumbled. "How is this happening?"

"How?" my mom spoke, giving me a baffled look. "I told you, honey. I'm always going to look after you. You're my daughter. I'm not going to let other people hurt you or ruin your life. Not Sabrina, not Travis, and not that disgusting Mr. Blouth."

"Mr. Blouth?" I questioned, tasting the salt of the tears that now stung my lips.

"That pig," my mom continued. "It was bad enough you were sneaking out of the house against my wishes, but to meet with *him*? Oh, you thought I didn't know? I knew. I followed you. I watched you with that pervert. You never could help yourself with older men, could you? Don't think I didn't notice you flirting with Detective Harrison. That's why I need to be there for you - to protect you against those sexual predators. And Mr. Blouth, he was the worst kind.

"You don't know this, but after you left him that night, some other girl showed up. He began professing his love to her like you didn't exist to him. *My* baby – not exist? How dare he! And then he placed his hand on her stomach and said he couldn't wait for the baby to be born. She was pregnant, Emma! He got her pregnant! Disgusting. He couldn't be allowed to live, abusing young girls like that.

"When that other girl ran off, I met him on the trail. I had some words with that man. Can you believe he had the nerve to call me crazy? Nobody calls me crazy. He brushed me off like he couldn't be bothered with me. He shoved me aside and walked past. I reached one hand into my jacket pocket, and with the other, I picked up a small rock and threw it at him. It hit him in the back of the head. That got his attention. He turned and yelled at me, *"What's wrong with you?"* Can you believe that? That pig thought there was something wrong with *me*. I bent down to pick up another rock, and he charged at me to prevent me from using it. I didn't. The knife I pulled out of my pocket worked better.

"It's funny, that blonde cheerleader had more fight in her than that grown-ass man. He crumpled to the ground into a fetal position after I stuck it to him only once. I watched him bleed. Then I stuck him a few more times for good measure. He'd never hurt my daughter – or any girl ever again.

"I left him there, not even thinking about covering anything up. Nobody would know. He was out at night. He got mugged. Shit happens. But then, none of it mattered once that bear smelled food. My little stab wounds got swallowed up in the jaws of that beast."

"No, no, no, no," I murmured, shaking my head in denial. "It's not true. Tell me it's not true."

She placed her hand under my chin to steady it so I could look her in the eye.

"When you become a mother," she said softly, "you'll understand. You'll do anything to protect your family. Anything. You are *my* daughter. You are Emma *frickin'* Murphy. And I won't let anybody hurt you."

She removed her hand from under my chin and swept her eyes around the room to take a final look.

"Nice place. Now let your mother take you out for something to eat."

She walked out into the hall and quietly waited. I stood in shock. Everything that happened

– it was all her. Everything I thought I knew was a lie. What was I supposed to do? She was my mom. I loved her. And everything she did was from a place of love. *Was it, though?*

I wiped the tears from my cheeks and closed my eyes. *Wake up! Wake up! Wake up!* I opened my eyes, hoping the nightmare would end, but I was still standing in the same spot, staring at my mother out in the hall.

"Come on, Emma, let's go," she waved me on.

I exhaled, forcing the contents of my stomach to stay down. All through my teenage years, I learned to keep secrets. I knew a fair share of them – some I wish I didn't know. Some I've used; most I've held onto. I thought it made me special. I wasn't special; I was hopeless. My mom was right; I needed her to protect me. And as long as I needed her, I'd file away at least one more secret. Like she said, *"You'll do anything to protect your family. Anything."*

I forced a smile and joined my mom out in the hall, closing the door behind me. Who knew she was so strong? I walked with her down the corridor, nervous, silent.., ready for another fresh start.

A LETTER FROM THE AUTHOR

Dear readers,

I hope you loved *Emma*. It wasn't a book I intended to write, but when my 14-year-old niece asked me if I could write a book about/for her, I couldn't resist. It took me a while to get into it, but once I did, I became excited and couldn't stop writing. I think she'll enjoy it.

And if *you* enjoyed it, I'd be very grateful if you'd consider writing a review. I love to hear what readers think, which helps me grow as an author, and it makes such a difference in helping new readers discover my books for the first time.

Check out my website at:

javo-publication.square.site

Where copies of all of my books (including signed copies) can be purchased. You can also find them on Amazon or ask your local bookstore to order them.

Thank you so much for your kind support!
Jeff

Enjoy these other great titles!

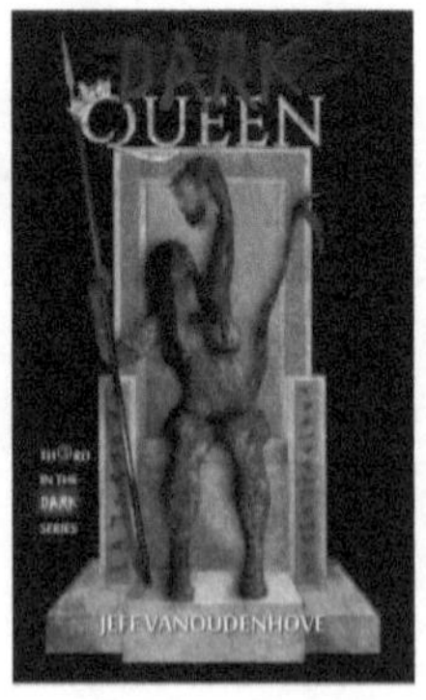

Jeff VanOudenhove has written several novels in the genre of dark fiction, including the **Dark Series,** a psychological thriller with supernatural elements, crime thrillers **The Alphabet Killer** and **The Letter Man**, the psychological suspense thriller **Just Listen**, and a book of truly twisted short stories, **Screams in the Dark and Other Twisted Tales**. His talent for storytelling combines unforgettable characters and dire situations, mixed with astonishing plot twists. **Emma** is Jeff's tenth book. He lives in Western Massachusetts with his wife, Elena.